THE HUSBAND SHE CAN'T REMEMBER

Southwest Secrets Series

TINA CAMBRIA

DEDICATION

This book is dedicated to all of my teachers, from first grade through graduate school. I'm grateful for everything I learned from them.

ACKNOWLEDGMENTS

Thank you to my husband Chris, who tirelessly supports and encourages me in everything I do.

Thank you to Susan Scott Shelley, a wonderful author and friend. Since I had the good fortune to meet her in an airport shuttle after a writing conference, Susan has been incredibly helpful in my efforts to launch my writing career. I sincerely appreciate all of the guidance and assistance she has provided.

A special thank you to Scott Spaulding, who designed a fantastic book cover for me.

CHAPTER ONE

She couldn't be pregnant!

Danielle Brinkworth shifted on the sofa. "Get real," she said, glaring at her best friend Leslie Martinson. "I have a lingering virus. A little more rest, and I'll be fine."

"Seriously, I think you're pregnant."

"I should've gotten a flu shot last winter." Danielle shrugged. "My mistake."

"A flu shot might not have been a bad idea," Leslie said, "but you need to take a pregnancy test."

"What on earth for?"

"To see if you're pregnant, of course." Leslie's brows pulled together. "Your nausea, lack of energy…and lately you've been complaining about tingly breasts. Those are classic signs of the early stage of pregnancy."

"Come on, I've pretty much done nothing but mope around your house for almost five weeks since I was released from the hospital." She'd always thought Leslie was a highly qualified nurse, but this conversation raised some doubts. Danielle lifted her chin. “You need a man to get pregnant, and I haven’t been with one.”

“Maybe not since your car accident, but what about the week before that?”

“Nothing happened in L.A., if that’s what you’re implying.” Danielle crossed her arms across her chest.

Leslie narrowed her eyes. “You don’t remember anything from the time you left L.A. until you regained consciousness after your accident. There’s a whole week of your life that’s unaccounted for.”

What was Leslie insinuating? That Danielle had somehow gotten pregnant on the trip from California back home to Colorado?

Yeah, right.

She’d never even been intimate with her former fiancé. Maybe she ought to remind Leslie of that. But why bother? Leslie would only start in about how Walter Ferguson had never been Danielle’s fiancé since there was no proposal, no engagement ring, and no wedding plans.

“Come on, Leslie. You know nothing’s happened between Walter and me.”

Leslie’s eyes lit up. “I guess I’d be shocked if you told me Walter had taken things to the next level, so to speak.”

“And he’s only stopped by here once since I’ve gotten back from L.A.” Danielle was a little embarrassed to admit that her so-called fiancé—or it would be more accurate to call him her former so-called fiancé—had barely attempted to make any kind of move on her in all the time she'd known him. Then again, she hadn't totally minded Walter being a little old-fashioned. A couple of her boyfriends back in college were just the opposite, and those relationships had flamed out after a few months.

"Just humor me, okay?" Leslie laughed, and then her face turned serious. "Hopefully, you've only got some minor virus. So, I'll pick up a pregnancy test, and we'll make sure that's not what's causing your symptoms."

"If that's what it takes to make you stop talking crazy talk, I'll pee on a little stick for you," Danielle said, letting out a huff. The test would turn out negative anyway. It was nothing more than a waste of money.

"Trust me," Leslie said. "It's a good idea.

Danielle didn't agree, but she owed Leslie big time. Her best buddy had let her stay at her house for five weeks while recuperating from the car accident. Leslie was beyond generous. So what if her biology knowledge was a little deficient for a nurse? It wouldn't hurt to simply play along and do the pregnancy test. Then when it turned out negative—as Danielle knew it would—she'd drink plenty of fluids and overdose on resting to knock out this pesky virus.

After Leslie left for the drugstore, Danielle settled on the sofa and tried to focus on a TV cooking show. Feeling a chill, she pulled a quilt from the back of the sofa to cover her tank top and pajama bottoms.

Pregnant? No way.

She'd spent six months in L.A. and hadn't strayed so much as an inch from the straight and narrow. In fact, some people would call her a prude for chucking her dreams because of what she'd been asked to do.

But why should she care what anyone thought of her? She'd given it her best shot. Nothing to be ashamed of. Still, her transformation from an energetic teacher and aspiring actress into a total couch potato had taken its toll on her outlook. How many other twenty-six-year-old women would spend five weeks mostly watching TV, flipping through magazines, and petting their best friend's dog?

None that she knew. And she was more than ready for a change. Stir-crazy was what her Nana would call it.

If only she didn't feel so…confused and worn-out—

She stopped herself. It was simply a matter of getting her energy back. And getting back her memories of that missing week. After that, she'd focus on a new dream.

Struggling to keep her eyes open, she gave in to sleep. She had no idea how much time had passed when the barks of Leslie's dog Ollie woke her. "What is it, boy?" Danielle sat up on the sofa to find the bulldog with his front paws on the living room windowsill. "What's out there?"

She draped the quilt over her shoulders and hurried to the window to see what was bothering the dog. "Must be that guy who's parked in front of the house," Danielle said, patting the growling bulldog on the head. "Is that what you're so excited about, Ollie?"

She spied a tall, dark-haired man emerging from a car and then pulling off a t-shirt to expose a muscular chest and powerfully-built arms to match. Now this was something she could get interested in. The tiniest bit of guilt trickled through her, but she quickly dismissed it. She was hardly violating the man's privacy by staring at him when he was the one standing shirtless on a public street.

Unable to look away, she watched the man retrieve a sport shirt from the back seat of the car, quickly put it on, and button it as he strode up Leslie's driveway. Danielle gulped at the air to calm her racing heart and then instinctively held her breath. The guy looked like he had urgent business to take care of.

She moved away from the window a second before the man stepped onto Leslie's porch and rang the bell. Now what? Answer the door to a stranger? An extremely good-looking and well-built stranger. But should his looks make a difference when there was a question of safety?

Curiosity won out over suspicion. "Who's there?" Danielle called out from behind the door.

"Danielle? Is that you?" a deep voice answered. "Please open the door."

Her friend's dog hopped up on his hind legs and scratched at the door. "Quiet, Ollie!" Danielle scolded. Or would the barks of the small bulldog be enough to scare away the stranger on the porch?

Her thoughts jumbled. This fellow had to know

her. How else would he know her name? After all, the doctors told her she had partial amnesia from the blow she'd probably taken to the head in the accident. He was most likely a forgotten friend from L.A. who'd been swallowed by that black hole of amnesia…

Cautiously opening the door, Danielle came face to face with over six feet of manly attractiveness. His brown eyes flew open wide when he saw her, and then he gave her a quick once-over.

"How do you know me?" she demanded. "Who are you?"

The man took a step back, recoiling as though he'd been slapped. "Danielle, what do you mean?" His jaw dropped, and his eyes narrowed in suspicion. "I'm your husband."

* * *

What was she trying to pull?

Granted, Kyle hadn't known her very long, and he hadn't seen her for over five weeks. But this was definitely Danielle. *His* Danielle. Danielle Brinkworth, of New Loudon, Colorado. Now Danielle Williams, his lawful wife.

The little bit of color in Danielle's face immediately disappeared. "My *husband*?"

"What's going on, baby?" Something was definitely off. She looked almost…ghostly. "You didn't forget me that quickly, did you?"

"I-I need to sit down," she stammered, and sagged sideways.

Kyle caught her, wrapping one arm under her knees and the other arm around her back. Gathering

Danielle into his arms, he gently carried her to the sofa and covered her with the quilt that had been covering her shoulders. A jowly bulldog followed them and barked again. That had to be her friend's dog Ollie, from Danielle's description of him. "Take it easy, Ollie," he said, quieting him with several strokes to the dog's head.

Danielle's eyelids fluttered, and confused-looking blue eyes stared back at him.

Tentatively stepping away, he shared in her confusion. He still had a hard time believing he'd flown all the way to Denver and then driven to New Loudon to track her down. But what else could he do? He hadn't been able to reach her by phone or text message since she'd headed off from Las Vegas, promising to contact him after she got back to Colorado.

"I haven't heard from you in weeks. You made me crazy-worried about you." Kyle pondered Danielle reclining on the sofa. For all he knew, she might have decided she wanted nothing more to do with him. It wouldn't be the first time a woman decided that. But it would be the first time a woman went so far as to actually marry him and then decided he wasn't the right man for her.

Her mouth fell open. "I don't even know what you're talking about."

Am I nuts for coming here?

It wasn't like him to chase down women who didn't answer his messages. And it definitely wasn't like him to spend a few hundred bucks for a flight, fly over two hours, and then drive another fifty miles from the airport in search of a woman who didn't answer his messages.

Except this one was his wife.

No, this sure wasn't the type of thing he would normally do. Not for any woman, no matter how silky her blond hair was, or how velvety her pale skin felt when he ran his rough hands over it—hold on, his mind had drifted to a place he didn't intend it to go.

Business came first. He and Danielle had a legal matter to settle, and that was his top priority. She was supposed to make a decision and finalize the paperwork. He'd agreed to accept whatever she decided, but first he had to find out what her decision was.

"Danielle, are you sick or something?" Kyle took in her pajama bottoms and tank top and checked the time on his cell phone to make sure it really was early afternoon. "Not to be rude, but why aren't you dressed at this time of day? You don't look like…yourself."

"I don't even know you. So, I can't imagine how you'd know what I usually look like."

Now he'd lost his patience. They'd made a deal. And the ball was in her court.

"Are you trying to pull a fast one on me?" Irritation bubbled up inside him. "I know I left you with options. And you have a big decision to make. But why are you trying to act like you don't even know me? Don't tell me you're ashamed of what happened."

"Do I have something to be ashamed of?" Danielle asked, her voice quivering.

"I guess that depends on your definition of

right and wrong." Kyle couldn't stop himself from grinning.

He pictured Danielle giving him a breezy wave as she drove off toward Denver from Las Vegas. As she'd smiled and pulled away, he would've sworn she would decide to continue their partnership.

And that's what Kyle wanted her to decide. Yeah, he had to admit it. He didn't want to end things with her. Now that he'd tracked her down, he didn't want her to sign those papers. What had started as a simple business deal had quickly gotten real complicated. But in a good way.

No, Kyle Williams wasn't one to run away from problems. He'd own up to that. Hell, he created enough of his own problems that it would be impossible to run away from them.

"Now you really have me worried," Danielle said. "Talking about right and wrong." She worked the edge of the quilt through her fingers. "Er, what did I do that someone might consider as wrong?"

Before he could answer, the front door opened. A woman stood in the doorway, taking in the scene. With her fists clenched on her hips and her chest thrust out, she reminded Kyle of a plainclothes version of Wonder Woman, but with a pixie haircut.

"Who are you, and what are you doing in my house?" she demanded.

Straightening his shoulders, Kyle stood and locked eyes with her. "I'm Danielle's husband, and I'm here because I haven't heard a word from her in over five weeks."

Now it was the Wonder Woman-wannabe's turn to have the color drain from her face. She slumped and released her hold on the small shopping bag she was carrying.

Kyle hurried across the room toward her. Two fainting women in one afternoon. What kind of weird place had he wandered into?

But the dizzy expression quickly passed from the woman's face, and she managed to right herself and turn to Danielle. "Do you know this guy?"

Danielle shook her head. "I-I don't remember him."

The woman assumed her superhero pose for a second time, and her voice turned challenging again as she faced Kyle. "You'd better get out of my house, or I'm calling the cops right now. Danielle's not married. To you or anybody else. I don't know what kind of game you're playing, but it's officially over."

"I've got the marriage certificate in my car if you'd like to see it." He matched her challenging tone as he bent down to retrieve the shopping bag she'd dropped. A box labeled "pregnancy test" spilled out of the bag as he picked it up. "What have we here?"

Neither woman said a word.

CHAPTER TWO

Pregnant.

Danielle stared at the word on the little stick. If the accuracy claims on the box were right, it was more than ninety-nine-percent sure that she was indeed pregnant. Those were pretty good odds.

But how? Well, she knew how. The birds and the bees and all that stuff.

But when? And with whom? Not that man outside the bathroom door waiting for her to give him the news. Exactly who was he, anyway?

She might not be able to remember what had happened during the time after she'd left L.A. until she'd wound up in a hospital in western Colorado a week later. But at least now she had an idea of one thing she'd done in the course of that missing week.

Oh, and she'd apparently married him too.

What did he say his name was? Or had he even said? Her thoughts bounced around like popcorn kernels in the microwave. He'd called out her name from the porch, and he'd claimed to be her husband after she'd opened the door. And then when he saw the box with the pregnancy test, he'd just assumed that she—and not her friend—was the one who needed to check whether she was pregnant. With his baby.

And it turned out he was right. About the pregnancy part, at least. But was he the father? If only she could recall how she met him. Or where they'd met. Was he really claiming that she'd married him?

Why couldn't she remember any of this?

His polite but persistent rapping at the powder room door pulled Danielle back into the here-and-now. She'd had less than a minute to try to make sense of the effect that word on the plastic stick would have on her life, and now this stranger was pressing her to share the news with him. "I'll be out in a minute."

"Don't keep me in suspense. What's the result?"

"Just a minute…" What the heck was his name? Here he was demanding to know the most personal details of her life, and she didn't have a clue who the guy was. Going strictly on his looks, she might not mind getting to know him better. On the other hand, for all she knew, he could be one of those clean-cut serial killers.

Strange modus operandi for a serial killer. Show up at the intended victim's door claiming to be her husband and then force her to take a pregnancy test. Wait—he'd somehow found out her name and shown up where she was staying. Then when Leslie arrived with the pregnancy test, he'd had a fifty-fifty chance of picking the right woman. But for what purpose?

And that still didn't explain how—according to that little plastic stick—she was pregnant when she couldn't even remember doing what was required to get that way.

"I'm coming right out," she said, trying to keep her tone light and breezy. Would he grab her and put a knife to her throat when she opened the powder room door? Had he already overpowered Leslie? She shouldn't have left her friend alone with him when he'd insisted he wasn't leaving until she took the pregnancy test.

Why had she even opened the front door to him?

If only her cell phone hadn't been demolished in the car accident. She should've replaced it by now. That way she could call 911 and get a patrol car over ASAP. But what would she tell the police officer? She'd opened the door to a man who was now forcing her to take a pregnancy test? A test that she'd been planning to take anyway.

Somehow—and exactly how was the million-dollar question—her hormones had told the chemicals in the test stick that a new life was forming inside of her.

"Danielle?" The rapping on the door began again.

She sucked in a gallon of air and opened the door. Her mystery man's eyes showed he was waiting for the answer to an important question. Shrugging, she held the plastic stick in front of her, so he could see the word that had appeared.

"This is epic," he said.

"I guess you could call it that." She couldn't stop the trembling that overtook her. "But in a good way…or what they call an epic fail?"

His eyes glinted, and he flashed a grin. "No failure here, darlin'." Nodding at the plastic stick in her hand, he said, "Looks like we scored a touchdown."

"Were we trying to?"

"What—start a family before the ink on our marriage certificate was barely dry? I don't think we were necessarily intending for that to happen." He paused and shot her a questioning look. "But maybe it's okay."

"Okay?" Danielle's voice rose. "How can it be okay when I don't even know you?"

She suddenly became aware of Leslie peeking around the stranger's shoulder. Avoiding eye contact, Danielle held out the stick so that Leslie could see the life-changing word now being displayed.

"I knew it," Leslie said.

Danielle made a mental note not to question Leslie's knowledge of human biology again. "Well, now what do we do?" she mumbled, talking more to herself than to anyone in particular.

"First thing we do is sit you down in the living room," Leslie said, pushing past the man, grabbing Danielle by the hand, and leading her to the sofa. "Then we schedule a doctor's appointment, so you can be examined, start taking prenatal vitamins, and all that good stuff."

"Are you always this bossy?" he asked Leslie, trailing behind the women into the living room.

"Excuse me, who are you anyway?" Leslie frowned at the man hovering over her best friend. "And I think the proper term is leadership skills."

"Kyle Williams." He smiled. "Sorry about not giving proper credit to your leadership abilities. And you are…?"

"Leslie Martinson. I'm Danielle's best friend," she said, protectively placing a hand on her friend's shoulder. "And the owner of this house."

"Nice to meet you." Kyle extended his hand. "Sorry I didn't recognize you from the photo Danielle showed me. As I mentioned before, I'm her husband."

Ignoring the offer of a handshake, Leslie shook her head and turned to Danielle. "Is that true?"

"I-I don't know," Danielle spluttered. She would have sworn under oath that she'd never seen the guy before. But she also would have sworn under oath that there was absolutely no chance at all that she could be pregnant. And yet, it looked fairly certain that she was. She'd have a doctor confirm it, of course. Still, between the symptoms and the test results—it was apparent that something momentous had happened during that week she couldn't remember.

"Look, what's going on here?" Kyle eased himself onto the sofa and took Danielle's chin into his hand. Looking deep into her eyes, he dropped his voice to a whisper. "I know you're damn good at pretending, but I don't get what this act is about."

A chill ran up Danielle's spine. She hadn't

known his name until he'd introduced himself a few minutes earlier. And she had no recollection of ever meeting Kyle Williams until today. But there was something…something she couldn't exactly describe, and it drew her to him.

He knew her name and had sought her out. He claimed to be her husband. And there was a pretty good chance that she was going to have a baby—maybe his. She didn't want to believe it, but there had to be some kind of connection between them. And she had to find out what it was.

"Leslie, could you please give us some time alone?" Ignoring the shocked expression on her friend's face, Danielle continued, "We have some things to discuss."

* * *

By the time Leslie reluctantly left, Kyle was more than ready to get to the bottom of why Danielle acted like she didn't know him. He'd had girls dump him before. But not like this.

No woman he'd been involved with had ever broken things off without giving him some kind of verbal send-off. Telling him off would be a better description. And he'd probably deserved it most of the time.

But claiming to not even know him? This was a whole new ballgame. And this woman had actually married him. There was definitely something totally different about the attractive young woman sitting next to him now.

"So, tell me what's up with acting like you never met me before, Danielle."

"I honestly don't remember ever meeting you," she said. "But that doesn't mean we haven't met."

"Haven't met? Believe me, we did a lot more than just meet." He sure couldn't forget the week they'd spent together. It wouldn't be much of a stretch for him to call it one of the best weeks of his life. Maybe even *the* best week of his life. And not just their lovemaking. He actually liked Danielle. Liked her a lot.

"I'm starting to believe that." She blushed. "I mean, if that pregnancy test is accurate, I must've done a lot more with…*someone*."

"Oh, it was me all right." Noting the flush of embarrassment spread through her face and neck, he patted her hand. "You didn't do anything wrong. We made it legal before anything happened."

"But why would I marry someone I barely knew?"

"You really don't remember?" Taking in her attire, he cleared his throat. "Look, I've been trying not to be rude, but you haven't told me why you're still in pajamas at this time of day. Something's not right with you, and it's got to be more than a bout of morning sickness."

"I was in a car accident about five weeks ago. On the last leg of my way home from California."

Kyle caught his breath. "Are you okay?'

"Mostly okay. My car was totaled." She moved her hands up and down her thighs. "I don't remember anything about it. And they said I lost consciousness for a few minutes afterwards."

"Sounds pretty serious." Anything that knocked somebody out was scary. "What happened?"

"An eyewitness saw a big SUV swerve from the right lane toward the median on I-70, near the Utah/Colorado line. The SUV clipped a car in the left lane, and that car bounced off the guardrail and fishtailed right in front of me."

"That's the car that hit you?"

She nodded. "Head-on."

"I don't know what to say." His gut clenched. "You were lucky you didn't get killed."

Why hadn't she contacted him? Maybe he wouldn't have been the first person she'd call in an emergency, but she should've let him know about an accident that serious.

"I guess the seat belt, shoulder harness, and air bag did their job. I ended up with a really nasty bruise from the shoulder harness and a pair of black eyes from the air bag." She tilted her head back and closed her eyes for a second. "Nothing broken, so I got off pretty lucky."

"But you don't remember any of this?"

She shook her head. "The doctors think I either bumped my head on the driver side window or suffered a mild concussion just from the force of the impact with the other car. Either way, the last thing I remember before the accident was leaving my apartment in L.A. and heading home. Back here, to Colorado."

What was she telling him? She didn't remember how they'd met in Barstow, California, cooked up a business deal on the way to Vegas, and turned it into the week of their lives? Or at least the week of *his* life?

No, he was willing to bet they'd both had the

week of their lives.

Kyle couldn't help arching an eyebrow. "So, this is some kind of temporary amnesia thing?"

"The doctors say it's amnesia—you've got that right. But they're hedging on the temporary part."

"And yet you know your name, people in your family…things like that?"

"Yes, thank goodness. It's not a global loss of memory." She managed a tentative smile. "I just can't remember anything from the time I set out from L.A. until I woke up in the ambulance on the way to the hospital. The doctors said it's a kind of partial amnesia associated with traumatic events."

"But there's a chance your memories might come back?" He touched her forearm. The soft feel of her skin brought back his memories of the week they'd spent together. Could she really not remember any of it?

"Maybe, maybe not." She sighed. "The neurologist said it's possible that something may trigger my memory, and it could all come back. Then again, he said I may never remember a single thing about that week."

He should probably tell her all the details of their time together. Their chance meeting, the deal they'd made, how a business arrangement had turned into a whole lot more. He'd be doing her a favor, wouldn't he?

If only he knew the effect that would have on her. Maybe he'd shock her so much that she'd also forget her name and everything else about herself. He sure wasn't a doctor and definitely was no expert on the intricacies of the brain.

But still… Now there was a baby involved. And he was certain that the baby was his. Could he convince Danielle that they'd shared something special during their time together?

CHAPTER THREE

Danielle tried not to stare at Kyle as they ate lunch an hour later at the Java Junkie Coffee Corner. She definitely liked what she saw.

Full-on gorgeous.

And they were married? Unless he'd gone to an awful lot of trouble to create a phony marriage certificate—complete with a raised government seal—it had become clear that they'd indeed gotten married in Las Vegas about six weeks earlier.

"So, run this by me again. My car broke down in Barstow, and you gave me a lift to Vegas?" She'd been there in mid-August. You'd think she'd remember her car conking out in a town where the summertime high temperature averaged around a hundred degrees. But nothing about it sounded familiar.

Kyle took a swig of iced coffee and nodded. "That's right. I came out of the convenience store next to the gas station. As I headed to my car, I heard you talking to the mechanic. You were bent out of shape because he said you needed a new fuel pump, and your car wouldn't be ready until sometime the next day."

"So, I just hopped into your car and let you drive off to Las Vegas with me?" This sounded so out of character for her. Her mother and grandmother had always told her not to accept rides from strangers. She must have been out of her mind.

"No, give yourself credit for having some common sense, Danielle." He smiled and gave her a conspiratorial wink.

The guy acted like they had a history together. Well, they obviously did, judging from the results of the home pregnancy test.

And when Kyle went on to tell her how he'd overheard her say to the mechanic that she had a non-refundable deposit for a hotel room in Las Vegas that night, Danielle couldn't help but believe him. Because she did remember pre-paying that deposit to stay one night in Vegas on her journey back home to Colorado. She'd made the arrangements the day before she'd left L.A.

Even though she had no recollection of him before he'd shown up at Leslie's door earlier, it didn't seem that hard to picture Kyle introducing himself and asking if he could provide any assistance, such as driving her to Vegas. Especially if he told her that he just happened to be heading there himself.

Kyle told her that when the mechanic mentioned that he also had plans to be in Vegas the next evening and offered to deliver her repaired car to a hotel on the Strip, the deal had been sealed.

It kind of made sense, didn't it? She supposed it could have happened.

"You're telling me I was some sort of an accidental hitchhiker, and over the course of a two-hour drive through the desert, we decided to get married?" That had to be one wild car ride. If he wasn't a smooth-talking salesman, he was in the wrong line of business.

"Actually, the decision to get married came a little later."

"Uh…how much later?"

Kyle set down his fork, leaned toward her, and dropped his voice. "Before our little one was conceived, if that's what you're worrying about. I already told you we made it legal first."

She shot him a look of exasperation. "The timing of the event actually isn't my biggest concern right now. The *why* of it is what I'm trying to figure out."

Looking at Kyle's strapping physique and chiseled features, it was a no-brainer that making love with him wouldn't be the worst thing she could imagine. But she wasn't the type to go in for one-night stands. Even if the one-night part of it turned into a full week.

And what about getting married? She was leaning towards believing that she'd accepted a ride to Vegas with Kyle. But married a man she'd just met? That part wasn't adding up.

Kyle glanced around the coffee shop and then looked squarely at her. "It was no more than a business deal at the outset. Plain and simple."

Could this get any worse? He couldn't be calling what she'd done a euphemism for…for something she was sure she'd never consider.

"Please tell me you're not talking about—" She stopped short when a familiar figure appeared in the doorway of the coffee shop.

Following her gaze, Kyle swiveled in his seat and glanced toward the entrance. He sized up the red-haired man approaching their table and said, "That must be your former so-called fiancé, Walter."

* * *

Kyle did a quick visual assessment of Walter Ferguson. Pretty much the way he'd pictured the dude. An average-looking guy with a slouching posture, Walter determinedly threw back his shoulders and jutted out his chin as he moved toward them. This was the guy who hadn't been able to pull the trigger on his relationship with Danielle. The guy who let a beautiful woman call him her fiancé for something like two years without doing anything to make it official.

No wonder Danielle had given up on that sham of a relationship and headed to California in search of something better.

Now, Walter strode across the coffee shop like he was ready to lay claim to his long-lost treasure.

Too late, man. Someone else already staked that claim. And made it his own.

Standing up, Kyle made a pre-emptive strike and offered his hand. "Hey, dude," he said, pumping Walter's fist with a little more strength than necessary. With at least a five-inch height advantage over the newcomer, he figured that would combine with his authoritative handshake to let Walter know who had the upper hand. He didn't usually pull that kind of stunt on smaller guys, but he was pissed at the dude for the way he'd treated Danielle in the past.

"I don't believe we've met," Walter replied, extricating his hand from Kyle's grasp and flexing it a few times.

Kyle half-smiled. The guy was probably trying to get the blood circulating through his hand again. "I'm Kyle Williams," he said. How he wanted to add that he was Danielle's husband. And that she was pregnant with his baby. But he wouldn't do that to Danielle. This wasn't the appropriate time to make that announcement.

Nodding dismissively at Kyle, Walter turned to Danielle. "I'm surprised to see you out and about. You've been pretty much housebound since your accident."

She fidgeted with the food on her plate. "Kyle thought it would be good for me to get out of the house."

Kyle smiled with satisfaction as Walter's eyes reflected his surprise. He could imagine the thoughts going through old Walter's head. Like wondering who the hell Kyle was and why he influenced Danielle's decisions about what she should be doing.

Keep wondering, Walt. You'll find out soon enough.

Quickly looking back and forth at the couple,

Walter focused on Danielle again. "Perhaps I could stop over to see you tonight?"

She tapped her fingers on the table. "Not sure. Give me a call first, okay?"

Walter turned back to Kyle. Kyle sat back down and took a long drink of his coffee. He could almost see in the other man's eyes the exact instant when the proverbial light bulb clicked on.

"Yeah, maybe I'll do that," Walter said. "Or not." His eyes blazed as he turned abruptly and headed out the shop door without ordering anything.

Kyle couldn't help grinning at Danielle. "Hope I didn't mess things up between you and Walter."

"How did you know that was Walter?" she demanded in a low voice.

He shrugged and extended his hands, palms up. "You told me all about him. When we were in Vegas."

"What did I tell you?"

Kyle scanned the shop to be sure no one nearby seemed to be listening to their conversation. "You said he'd been your make-believe fiancé for about two years."

"Make-believe?" A faint blush crept up her neck. "I told you about that?"

"That's right. Maybe you said unofficial instead of make-believe, but let's call it what it was." Kyle picked up his coffee and took another swig. "No proposal, no engagement ring, no…getting it on."

"How dare you—"

"What?" Kyle cut in. "Am I saying anything that isn't true?" At her wounded look, he felt a pang of guilt. He didn't intend to hurt her. Or shame her. But Walter for sure had issues of his own, and Kyle doubted the guy would've ever made the next move. From what Danielle had told him back in Vegas, Walter was more concerned with pleasing his mother than making a real life with Danielle. He still couldn't fathom why she'd been interested in the guy as more than a friend.

Kyle reached across the table and covered her hand with his own. "I'm sorry. I didn't mean to be so cold." It had become clear that he needed to share the details of their week together more sparingly.

According to Danielle, she didn't remember anything about their whirlwind marriage and honeymoon. And she'd just found out a few hours before that she was pregnant. The way he saw it, two giant surprises had just landed in her lap in a flash.

Make that three. Because on top of finding out she'd married a virtual stranger and become pregnant on their honeymoon, she was suffering from some kind of amnesia and probably wasn't sure whether to believe what Kyle was telling her or not.

He needed to take things slow. Win back her trust. More than that, make her fall in love with him again.

He'd done it before. He could do it again, couldn't he?

There was even more at stake now.

Their baby.

* * *

After Kyle paid the lunch bill, Danielle walked with him to his rental car. Once settled inside, she turned to him and cocked her head. "Are you always that blunt?"

"Yeah, I guess you could say that. Although *blunt* is probably one of the nicer ways some folks have referred to me."

Danielle wondered who had described him in less favorable terms. A former girlfriend? Kyle apparently knew a lot about her personal history. He might have shared some of his background with her during that week she couldn't remember. For all she knew, there could be a line of women stretching half-way across Nevada, all waiting to take a swing at him.

What if one of those women were pregnant with his baby too? Good heavens, what had she gotten herself into?

"Do you have any children?" she suddenly blurted out.

A smile played at his lips. "None except this little one," he laughed, lowering his gaze and pointing his index finger at her abdomen.

"You seem to be so sure this is your baby."

"A hundred-percent sure."

"Under the circumstances, I'm surprised you don't insist on DNA testing."

"No need, darlin'."

She sniffed. "Well, maybe I should insist on it."

He shot her that disarming grin again. "Unless you hooked up with some stranger at a truck stop right after we parted in Vegas, I don't think there's any need for that."

"How can you be so sure?" He was certainly full of himself. Danielle mentally added the word *cocky* to the list of terms probably used to describe Kyle Williams.

"Be honest. Have you been…intimate…with any other man since you've been back here in New Loudon?"

She squirmed in the passenger seat. "I guess you mean with Walter?"

"No one but."

Staring straight ahead, her stomach knotted. Damn that Kyle Williams! He thought he was so smart. How did he know so much about her personal business?

"You know I've been recuperating from a serious car accident…"

"Now don't take this the wrong way," he said, "but you told me you got two black eyes and a big bruise on your chest from the accident. Plus, the memory loss." He brushed his hand across her cheek. "I'll bet that doctor in the Emergency Department didn't tell you to avoid sex for the next month or so."

The touch of his hand on her face burned, shooting a spark straight through her core. "What are you implying?"

"You and Walter have never made love." He traced a line across her lips with his index finger. "And you're never gonna, now that I'm in the picture."

She fumed inside as Kyle headed the car

toward Leslie's place. Within two minutes, he parked in front of the house, with Danielle still struggling to respond to his accusation. "What do you want from me, anyway?"

He cut the ignition and turned to her. "Look, I know you don't remember it, but we had a deal. Our marriage was part of it. It was supposed to be strictly business." He took another long look at her abdomen. "But as you figured out a little while ago, it ended up going farther than that. I guess you could say we went a little too far with our play-acting."

"And I ended up pregnant…" she whispered.

"Exactly. That wasn't part of the original plan." His lips twitched. "But we were considering Plan B anyway when we parted ways in Vegas. That's why I'm here—to find out what you decided."

"Plan B?"

What was he referring to? She was an ordinary small-town high school teacher. Granted, she'd taken a short break from teaching English and drama to pursue her lifelong dream of becoming a professional actress. And when that hadn't worked out, she'd headed back home, hoping to get her old job back for the fall term.

This stranger expected her to believe that he'd given her a lift across the Mojave Desert and somehow gotten her tangled up in a scheme that included a sham marriage—and how make-believe was it if they'd actually consummated it? If only something would prompt the return of her memory. She definitely had been out of her mind when she'd agreed to whatever it was he'd proposed as part of his scheme.

"Yeah, Plan A was the fake marriage for a week and then a quick annulment. But then we got talking about Plan B—keeping it going for real."

"You mean…you mean we were actually falling in love?"

He chuckled. "You tell me, darlin'. I know I thought it was pretty special."

After all those years waiting for Walter to get serious about marriage, she'd found a man and fallen in love in a week's time? And she couldn't even remember anything about it.

Her heart thudded. She was sure it was going to jump right into her throat. This was too much to take in. And it didn't sound like anything she'd normally do.

Taking a calming breath, she weighed her options. Believe this guy outright? But maybe he *was* a whiz with creating fake government documents. And how hard would it be to find out a few facts about her? These days, you could learn almost anything about anyone on the internet in a matter of minutes.

Even if he were some kind of scam artist, why would he go after her? She didn't have a lot of money. If this was part of a trick, he'd sure gone to a lot of trouble to convince her that they were husband and wife.

"Do you have any proof that we were together, other than that marriage certificate?" Danielle asked.

His eyes lit up, and he pulled his phone from his pocket. He tapped it a few times, and then handed it to her. “Would this do it for you?”

She gasped when she saw the image on the screen. Was he here to blackmail her?

At least now she could believe that the act that had resulted in her pregnancy had probably taken place with Kyle. Squinting to take in all of the details, she could tell the photo was a selfie taken by him. Although her breasts were mostly covered with water, she was apparently topless in what appeared to be a hot tub. With Kyle beside her. With each of them holding what looked like a glass of champagne in their hand. And with big smiles on both of their faces.

“I-I don’t remember this,” Danielle stuttered. Still, she had a pretty good idea what could have happened shortly after that picture was taken.

“Our wedding night,” he said, giving her a playful wink.

CHAPTER FOUR

Danielle put a hand to her chest, as if that would slow the frenzied pounding of her heart. She knew all about Photoshopping pictures, but Kyle would have to be some kind of creative genius to create that image if she'd never actually been in a hot tub with him.

And hadn't most likely been naked. Or at least half-naked.

"Could I see that photo again?" She clasped his phone and confirmed there was something that looked like a wedding band on the third finger of her left hand. "So, this was *after* our wedding ceremony?"

He laughed. "I sure hope it wasn't before or during the ceremony. Would've been a little too up close and personal for my liking if the justice of the peace were squeezed in there with us."

Even though her heart was still racing, she couldn't help smiling. She didn't know much about

Kyle, but she liked his sense of humor. "I asked because I notice that I seemed to be wearing a wedding ring in that picture. And…well, I'm not wearing it now."

"That was how we left things. You gave it back to me at the end of the week. Said if you decided we should keep the marriage going for real…if you wanted to make it genuine and not just a business arrangement, you'd let me put the ring back on your finger."

"So, you have that actual ring?"

Kyle took his phone from her, pocketed it, and reached into the glove compartment. Danielle's mouth gaped open as she watched him pull out a small velvet pouch and tug on the string. With one hand, he opened her palm and with the other, he lightly shook the tiny pouch. She drew in a quick breath as a white-gold band with a row of small diamonds fell out into her hand.

"There it is, darlin'." He smiled and gave her that disarming wink. "Try it on if you'd like. I guarantee it fits you."

If her heart continued much longer at a breakneck pace, she was afraid it would pop right through her chest. He was sure doing a good job of making it look like they'd gone through a wedding ceremony and had an exciting wedding night. Unless he was a world-class con artist, his story was pretty convincing.

"But *why* would I have married a stranger? And managed to get pregnant in the process?" She stared at the diamond band in her palm as though it would reveal the answers to her questions. Even if he'd so easily convinced her to make love with him, she surely would have asked him to use protection. In fact, there was absolutely no reason why she wouldn't have demanded it. She'd never been the type to be swept away by uncontrolled desire.

Kyle's eyes flicked over her. "Are you ready to hear all of the details? And put that ring back on your finger?"

As much as she wanted to know what had happened in Vegas, she wasn't sure she was ready to hear it from Kyle.

Start remembering that week!

Why couldn't she command her brain to work the way it was supposed to? She wasn't asking to remember every trivial detail of that week in Las Vegas. What she ate for breakfast, the daily high temperatures, the brand of toothpaste she'd used—none of those things mattered to her now.

No, she just wanted to remember what had motivated her to sidetrack from her journey home and agree to spend a week with a complete stranger. And apparently marry him as part of the deal. And how she'd allowed herself to end up with a baby on the way. Even though Kyle offered to spell everything out for her, could she trust his explanation? She barely knew him. Maybe if he shared merely a detail or two, it would trigger her memory?

"I don't want to try it on." She held out her hand for Kyle to retrieve the diamond band. It seemed like some kind of bad luck to try on a wedding ring that wasn't her own. Even if maybe the ring *was* her own. But first she had to determine the circumstances surrounding how and why that ring was purchased.

"You're right." Kyle slipped the ring back into the velvet pouch. "No trying on unless you're ready to wear it for good. I already know it fits you."

She had to admit the sparkly ring looked extremely appealing. And yet she certainly would never have entered into the arrangement Kyle described solely for a piece of jewelry.

"I'm almost scared to ask…but we ended this supposed business deal with you keeping that diamond ring until I decided that we would stay married?"

"*If*, Danielle…if." He nodded and shot her his trademark grin again. "You were supposed to make your decision and get back to me. But I never heard from you."

"And you had no way of knowing I'd been in that car accident."

"Right. I kept calling your cell and getting your voicemail. So, it looked like you were blowing me off."

Danielle pictured the smashed-up mess of stainless steel, glass, battery, wires, and other phone components that the police had returned to her in a zipper storage bag. That was all that was left of her cell phone after it had gone airborne from its resting place in her car's drink holder. It wasn't cheap to replace a cell phone before the contract was up, and she'd managed to get along without it since the accident. How was she supposed to know there was an unknown husband out there who'd been trying to call her?

"So, if you thought I was done with you, why did you come all the way here to track me down?" She couldn't imagine what kind of explanation he'd have for that.

"We're married, remember?"

"Actually, I don't."

Kyle frowned. "Sorry, I guess this isn't the time for sarcasm about not remembering things. What I should have said is that if you don't want to stay married to me, we need to annul this thing. And I can't do that on my own."

Too many decisions to make.

She'd only just met the guy, and she had to decide if she wanted to remain married to him. And what about their baby? She didn't even have to think about whether she was going to keep it. Even though she'd only found out about the baby a few hours earlier, Danielle had already developed a maternal attachment to it.

"I need some time to think," she said to Kyle. "This is way too much to process in such a short time."

"I have to catch a 3 PM flight from Denver International tomorrow." His eyes sparkled. "But I'm all yours until I have to head to the airport."

All hers? She hoped he wasn't expecting a replay of their wedding night.

"Kyle, if you don't mind my asking, where are you staying tonight?"

He cleared his throat. "Seeing as I had no idea whether or not you might welcome your long-lost husband with open arms, I didn't make any arrangements for tonight."

"I see."

"Got any suggestions?"

"There's a hotel just off the interstate. You probably drove right past it on your way into town."

His mouth formed a small circle, and he let out a long exhale. "I could check it out and see if they have a room available tonight."

"I think that would be the best thing."

Even though she'd said it, she wasn't really sure at all that Kyle staying at the hotel off the interstate tonight would be the best thing. But it was probably the most sensible thing.

* * *

So, maybe he hadn't expected Danielle to welcome him right into her bedroom. But Kyle sure hadn't bargained for a complete erasure of him from her mind.

Before he could figure out what to do next, Leslie emerged from her house. Dressed in hospital scrubs, she ran down the driveway toward the car.

Seeing her wildly waving her arms, Kyle rolled down the window, expecting her to start shouting that her house was on fire.

"I'm glad you finally got back," she gasped, leaning into the car window opening and looking straight at Danielle. "I pulled some strings and got you an appointment with Dr. Chartoff this afternoon. He can see you in thirty minutes."

"What's the rush?" Danielle asked.

"To confirm that you're pregnant." Leslie eased herself back and stood at the curb, turning her gaze to Kyle. "Of course, it won't establish who the father is, but at least we'll know for sure if that at-home pregnancy test was accurate."

Kyle looked at Danielle, now shrinking into the passenger seat and staring at her lap. Man, she just kept getting hit with one shocker after another. Was this Dr. Chartoff even her regular doctor? Her friend, Leslie, had gone a little overboard with those so-called leadership skills she'd been referring to earlier, in his opinion.

"Are you okay with seeing the doctor this afternoon?" he asked Danielle.

She sighed. "I guess I need to visit a doctor at some point. So, if Leslie pulled some strings for me, I may as well take advantage of the appointment."

Kyle caught Leslie in his peripheral vision and turned to see her leaning through the car window opening again, looking at Danielle.

"Honey, I'm so sorry I can't come with you," she said to Danielle. "I have to leave for my shift at the hospital in a few minutes. Will you be all right without me?"

Clenching his jaw, Kyle paused before saying something he might regret. How had Leslie become Danielle's pregnancy coach? *He* was the baby's father, after all.

"I can be there with her," he said.

Leslie's eyes widened. "Certainly not during the doctor's examination!"

He checked himself before he almost asked Leslie whether she thought he'd be seeing anything he hadn't seen before. Even though he knew the answer to the question, it would be rude to say it in front of Danielle. And he didn't want to embarrass her. She'd been through enough that day.

"I can stay in the waiting room if that's what Danielle wants."

Turning back to Danielle, his heart wrenched as he noticed her trembling. "Are you all right, baby? Don't worry, I'll be there for you."

Her eyes met his, and he couldn't tell whether he saw fear or appreciation. If it was fear—well, what did he expect? She'd pretty much been minding her own business when he'd interjected himself into her life. Sure, she'd stood to benefit from the deal he had proposed to her. But neither one of them could have predicted they'd be sitting here six weeks later talking about getting a prenatal checkup. If that's what they called this type of doctor visit. This was all new territory for him.

When she pulled at his hand and didn't let go, his analysis of her mood leaned more toward appreciation. If she was afraid, she didn't seem to be afraid of *him*. Maybe just afraid of the situation she was in. And as far as the appreciation went—she most likely didn't appreciate that he'd gotten her pregnant. Probably just glad that she didn't have to go to the doctor's appointment alone. So, he'd be there for her and make sure she didn't feel like she was facing this all by herself.

"Thanks for setting up the appointment," Danielle said to her friend. "Kyle can drive me over there."

Leslie turned to Kyle. "You know, this mystery husband story—"

"There's no mystery," he said.

"Maybe not to you." Leslie rubbed her jaw.

"How did you know where to find Danielle?"

"When we were on our honeymoon—"

"Honeymoon?" Leslie's eyes widened.

"Yes, our honeymoon." Kyle nodded. "When we parted—temporarily—she said she'd be staying with her best friend for a while until she figured things out. She told me your name. And these days, once you've got someone's name and town, the internet makes it easy to find their address."

"What was she supposed to figure out?"

"Excuse me, Leslie, but some things are best kept between husband and wife." Kyle cocked his head and stared hard at her.

"You barely know her."

Danielle, who'd been sitting quietly in the passenger seat, leaned across him toward Leslie. "It's okay, sweetie. I'll be all right."

Looking back and forth at Danielle and Kyle, Leslie nodded. "Dr. Chartoff's office is on the second floor of the medical office building across from the hospital. I'll see you after I get home from work tonight," she said to Danielle, then turned and headed to her car.

With Danielle already gripping his right hand, Kyle placed his other hand on top of hers and gave it a squeeze. "Hey, we're in this together, right?" He smiled at her, and she managed a weak smile in return.

So, why did he now feel that he was trying to convince himself that they were a real couple as much as he was trying to prove it to Danielle?

* * *

Thirty minutes later, Danielle clutched the opening of a paper gown, trying to completely cover her chest while waiting on an examination table in Dr. Chartoff's office. Was it a mistake to bring Kyle into the room with her? She couldn't help shaking her head. What was the difference now? She seemed to be on a roll with making mistakes. Letting the man who claimed to be her husband sit with her during a GYN exam probably wasn't the biggest mistake she'd made in the past six weeks anyway.

"You all right?" Kyle leaned over from the chair next to the exam table and rubbed her forearm.

She bit her lower lip. "I guess."

They sat in silence, Kyle stroking her arm while she focused on remaining calm.

It was just a matter of finding out whether that at-home pregnancy test was accurate, right? But deep down she knew that if Dr. Chartoff confirmed the result, her whole life was going to change—probably in ways she couldn't even imagine.

The way the pregnancy would affect her body was the most obvious change to be expected. And see-sawing emotions too. She'd heard all about pregnant women feeling on top of the world and then going on a crying jag the next minute.

And, of course, she'd be concerned about the baby's health. She'd only found out about the baby a few hours earlier, and she already felt connected to it. She wanted to take good care of herself during the pregnancy to help ensure everything would be right with the baby.

Catching sight of a poster on the wall that laid

out the baby's development during each month of the pregnancy, thoughts of labor and delivery popped into Danielle's head. With the kind of luck she'd been having lately, she'd probably be one of those women who experienced twenty-four hours of hard labor.

And after that—there'd be an infant to care for.

All by herself.

Unless she worked something out with this guy sitting beside her. She sure wasn't going to agree to stay married to him just so she wouldn't have to raise a baby on her own. But how could she hold down a full-time job and take care of a baby without any help? Being a single mom was something she'd never expected to experience.

A light tapping sounded on the door to the exam room, and Dr. Chartoff entered with his nurse following behind. He introduced himself, shaking hands with Danielle and then with Kyle.

"I understand you're a brand-new patient, and you're here to confirm your pregnancy?" the doctor began.

Nodding, Danielle couldn't help thinking that Dr. Chartoff looked not much older than she was. If that. Quite a difference from her previous physician, a kindly silver-haired gentleman who'd retired from medical practice about a year earlier.

Explaining what he was doing as he proceeded, Dr. Chartoff listened to her heart and lungs with a stethoscope, examined her breasts, and then performed a pelvic exam. Although she hardly knew Kyle, Danielle found herself feeling grateful that he held her hand throughout the entire process.

When the doctor finished his exam, he instructed Danielle to sit back up on the table. He smiled. “My examination along with the lab work we did when you first arrived confirms what you suspected. Congratulations to both of you! Everything looks good so far, and I expect that you’ll become parents around May 8th of next year.”

So, it was really happening. She didn’t have any kind of energy-sapping virus, and the at-home pregnancy test had been accurate.

Danielle thought she heard Dr. Chartoff say something about a prescription for prenatal vitamins and scheduling a follow-up appointment for the next month, but his voice was muffled by a roaring sound that erupted in her head. She was going to have a baby. And the man at her side was probably the father.

But she barely knew him.

The roaring sound subsided enough for Danielle to hear Dr. Chartoff’s final piece of advice before he left the room. “Since you have no history of miscarriage and you haven’t experienced any bleeding thus far, there’s no reason why you can’t keep up your usual sexual activities for the time being,” he said, tucking his stethoscope into the pocket of his lab coat.

Usual sexual activities?

She wanted to call out for Dr. Chartoff to come back in the room, so she could explain that she and Kyle didn’t have any usual sexual activities. But she could imagine the expression on the doctor’s face—and on his nurse’s—when she said she’d married a man in Vegas who she didn’t even know and then must have had unprotected sex with him at least once.

And she didn't remember one bit of it.

Of course, she'd written down on the medical history form about her car accident and the resulting partial amnesia. But she'd left out one itsy-bitsy part of her story. The fact that their marriage had only taken place a week before the accident and was apparently part of some business scheme. Would anything really be gained by sharing that juicy bit of information with the doctor and his staff?

Dr. Chartoff knew she'd been in a car accident after the baby was conceived, so Danielle was happy to leave out the details about the week before that and avoid any potential judgment regarding her…her so-called extra-curricular activities in Vegas.

Looking over to Kyle after the doctor left the room, she wasn't sure how to take the pleased expression on his face. Was he happy to hear that everything looked good with the pregnancy? Or was he filled with eager anticipation after getting a green light from the doctor for more of what had gotten her in this condition in the first place?

CHAPTER FIVE

Kyle tried to figure out his next step after he and Danielle left the doctor's office and headed back to Leslie's house. Danielle acted like someone who'd just been told they'd hit the lottery. Mostly stunned and with a touch of nausea about to break through. And a big helping of fear of the unknown served up on the side.

"I guess that was a lot to take in," he said once they were inside the house. "No doubt about the baby now."

"What time is it?" Danielle asked, fanning herself with her hand. Before Kyle could even pull out his phone, she continued, "It couldn't have been more than a few hours ago that I thought I was laid low by some lingering virus. Now, a bona fide obstetrician has confirmed that I'm definitely pregnant. And I don't even know how it happened."

Kyle raised his brows. "Come on, Danielle. You do know how it happened…"

"You know what I mean." She winced and plopped onto the sofa, her expression changing to one of pure frustration. "I know I was running short on cash when I left L.A. And there's no denying that you're a good-looking guy."

"If you say so."

"But I just can't imagine how I would've gotten into a scheme that ended up with…with me getting pregnant."

On a typical day, Kyle was pretty sure she never would have done anything like what he'd convinced her to do. But things between them were anything but typical. Amnesia side effects or not, he had to tell her a little bit more about what had happened when they met. He could see she was torn up inside because she wasn't sure if she'd done something truly wrong—even illegal.

"Look, you didn't do anything wrong—"

"According to Dr. Chartoff, I did."

"When did he say you did anything wrong?" He'd been in the exam room with Danielle the whole time, and he'd be damned if he remembered hearing the doctor passing judgment on her.

She grimaced. "He didn't have to say it. I mean, he doesn't even know the circumstances of our so-called marriage."

"Why are you calling it a so-called marriage?" Irritation flared within him. "Maybe we didn't have two hundred guests and a five-tier wedding cake, but it's just as legal. It's for real, baby."

"It sounds like fraud to me. You said we were planning all along for a quick annulment."

Letting out a long sigh, Kyle rolled his eyes to

the ceiling. She had a point. “Okay, maybe it didn’t start out like a fairy tale. But how many marriages do? Everything isn’t always like in the movies.”

“So, how did you rope me in?”

“Geez, don’t make yourself sound like a calf running around a rodeo ring.” Besides, she hadn’t been that hard to rope in. Once he’d gotten the ball rolling, she’d been more than willing to go along with his idea.

Her chin rose. “Look, I think you owe me an explanation of how I got to be your wife and now—I guess—the mother of your child.”

He couldn’t disagree. Considering she had amnesia about that week, he did owe her an explanation of how she’d gotten into her present situation. A big explanation. But he needed to start slowly.

“You’re right.” He shook his head in agreement. “Let’s see—where should I start?”

“How about telling me how we went from you giving me a ride after my car broke down to us ending up half-naked in a hot tub?”

Grinning, he said, “Oh, we weren’t *half*-naked.”

“You’re not making this any easier, Kyle.”

He watched as a flush of color worked its way up her neck and into her cheeks. Time to dial down his descriptions a notch or two. Even though he enjoyed thinking back to their week in Vegas, Danielle’s head obviously wasn’t in the same place. And how could it be? Some kind of force to her brain had wiped out those memories.

But she’d feel the same way as he did about

what they had shared if she could just remember it, wouldn't she? He sure hadn't needed to strong-arm her into marrying him or making love with him. Granted, she had training in acting. But she'd be up for an Academy Award if she'd only been acting like she was having a good time with him that week.

No, everything they'd shared had been the real deal. He'd be willing to bet on it.

Kyle patted her hand. "I apologize if I'm embarrassing you. That wasn't my intention."

"Apology accepted." She nodded, and a tentative smile seemed close to emerging. "So, can you tell me more about what happened after you gave me a ride? And clarify exactly when this idea of getting married was hatched?"

He recapped how he'd stopped at a convenience store in Barstow, California on his way to Las Vegas from L.A. "It was a pit stop to use the restroom and pick up a cold bottle of water. I was strictly being a Good Samaritan when I offered to give you a ride to Vegas, so you wouldn't lose your hotel deposit."

"And being a Good Samaritan included marrying me?" Danielle asked, her voice practically oozing skepticism.

"Now hold on, you're getting ahead of the story." He needed to tread carefully but still stick to the truth. "I had no plans to marry you—or sleep with you—when I offered you the ride. I mean, I thought I would *like* to sleep with you, but—"

"*But* what?"

"But I'm a gentleman," Kyle said. "Seriously, I

am. I didn't intend to act on my desires."

"And just when did you decide to forget about being a gentleman?"

Kyle decided to ignore the thinly-veiled insult. "Like I said, not until we said our vows, and that wedding ring was on your finger."

She huffed out a sigh. "This just keeps going in circles."

"Whoa, let's regroup here." Kyle held his palms in front of him. "I was on a business trip. But I've gotta admit that when I tell you what it was about, you may think it sounds a little shady."

"Could this get any worse?" Danielle moaned.

"Let me finish." He'd better make his explanation good or he was liable to lose Danielle before he ever got the chance to let her get to know him again. "My boss had given me what he called an important assignment to gather information on a competitor—an upscale resort that just opened in Vegas and caters to honeymoon couples."

"You mean working there and learning how they operate behind the scenes?"

"In hindsight, that might have been a better strategy. But no, my boss had something more dramatic in mind."

"Just spit it out, please."

Kyle took a deep breath. He felt like he was one step away from jumping off the high dive—into an empty pool. "My boss came up with the idea for a female colleague and me to check into the resort posing as husband and wife. Going undercover as guests to observe how things were done there. He lined up a woman who worked in management at our Scottsdale location."

Danielle gaped at him. "You're kidding, right?"

He shook his head. "I said *undercover*, not under the covers. We were going to keep it one-hundred-percent platonic in the bedroom. Just act…you know…all romantic when we were at the pool, having dinner, or any place where people could see what we were doing."

"And the female co-worker agreed to this?"

"Well, she did at first. I mean, it seemed like an opportunity to get a big raise or a promotion."

"But she changed her mind…"

Kyle shot her a thumbs-up signal. "Exactly. While you were settling your car repair arrangements with the mechanic, I got a text from her saying she was sorry, but she couldn't go through with it."

"So, you got the bright idea to substitute me in for that other woman."

Kyle laughed. "You're making me out to be a much quicker thinker than I actually am."

Noting the slightest trace of a grin, he knew he had the chance to soften Danielle's impression of what had happened when they'd made their deal. Besides, they hadn't done anything wrong. At least that's what he'd been trying to convince her. Because that's what he believed. Everything was legal.

They had nothing to regret. But what about their baby? That little one put a whole new wrinkle into their business arrangement. No more signing a piece of paper and forgetting that the whole week had ever happened. Actually, because of her car accident, Danielle had already forgotten that the whole week had ever happened. But the baby growing inside her was going to be an undeniably tangible reminder of what had taken place.

He launched back into his explanation. "I didn't say anything about the text message or even why I was heading to Vegas at first. And I didn't need to fill in any awkward silences. You opened right up about why you were driving to Vegas and then on to Colorado."

Danielle's voice was barely audible. "What did I tell you?"

"The whole thing about leaving your teaching job to try to make it big in Hollywood as an actress. How you thought you were finally getting a break after six months when you landed a small part in a movie."

"And I told you what happened when filming started?" she whispered.

He nodded. "Yeah, you were crushed when you showed up and found out your big part consisted of you lounging in a pool naked, sprawled out in one of those floating lounge chairs."

She sniffled. "It was humiliating. There was no acting involved. Just showing off my breasts for the whole world to see."

She looked so vulnerable, like a pretty cloth doll tucked into a corner of the sofa. It reminded him of the way she'd looked when she was slumped into the passenger seat of his Explorer as they traveled across the desert, telling him about throwing in the towel on her acting dream.

Putting an arm around her, Kyle said, "But you

didn't bare your breasts for the camera. You told me that once you found out what the job was really about, you walked out. And decided you'd had enough of trying to be a Hollywood actress."

"But then I showed off my breasts for you. You have the photo on your phone to prove it. And it sounds like I might have done it for money."

"Baby, we were married when that picture was taken."

"And tell me again how that happened. Or tell me for the first time, because I still don't think I've got the whole story."

"We headed from Barstow toward Vegas and, like I said, you told me about trying to break into acting in Hollywood. We got to commiserating. I told you about the insane job assignment I was on and how it was going all wrong. We kind of hit it off." His face lit up. "I mean, in a strictly-friends kind of way."

"I'm glad we at least liked each other."

"Oh yeah, we did. And we had something in common—dreams getting crushed and all that."

"Hollywood can be a dream-crusher, that's for sure," she said, resignation showing in her voice.

"The business world can sometimes do a pretty good job of crushing dreams too. I've gotten a couple of bruises along the way."

"Sounds like we bonded while we were driving." She looked at him with questioning eyes.

"I'd say that." He grinned. "Then—boom! I suddenly got this idea that maybe you could fill in for that woman in management from Scottsdale. What with your acting experience…well, I figured you'd be a natural."

Should he tell her that he'd also figured it wouldn't be that hard for him to pretend he was having a good time with a beautiful new wife? Because Danielle pretty much fit the bill for the kind of woman he'd conjure up as a potential wife if he'd been putting together the specifications. No, better to leave the physical attraction part of the equation out of the discussion right now.

"So, it was basically an acting job. Spend a week at a resort pretending to be your wife and get paid for it."

"You got it. Nothing funny going on in the bedroom. Put a wall of pillows down the middle of the king-sized bed, and nothing but sweet dreams every night."

Her face tightened. "This resort you were scoping out required a marriage certificate before they'd let us check in?"

"Hell, no." He couldn't believe what he'd just heard. "What kind of hotel asks for that in this day and age? And in Vegas, of all places."

"Then why'd we actually get married? Couldn't we just pretend? I *am* an actress, after all."

He shot her a grin. "Maybe that desert air does something to people's thought processes. I don't know. You were flipping through the resort brochure while we were driving, looked at a picture of their wedding chapel, and made a joking remark about us getting married so I could report back to my boss on how they handled marriage ceremonies."

"And you took it seriously?"

"I guess we both got a little giddy. Something was happening that was kind of…special."

"That desert air sounds a little dangerous."

"Sometimes people find danger kind of exciting," he said, locking eyes with Danielle.

"Sometimes people regret things that felt exciting at the time…"

He was tempted to point out that sometimes people regret never doing things that might have been exciting, but he checked himself. "People see things different ways."

Her voice took on the tone of a prosecuting attorney. "And how was I going to get paid for this charade?"

Kyle fidgeted next to Danielle on the sofa. "Out of my pocket. I figured if I gathered enough good information on the competitor for my boss, I'd easily recoup the money in a bonus or a promotion."

"How much was my payment?"

He locked eyes with her. "Five grand."

"Holy crap. That's serious money."

"Damn serious. Which is why I was so surprised that you never cashed my check."

* * *

Upstairs in the guest room a few minutes later, Danielle rooted through the top drawer of the dresser she'd been using while staying with Leslie.

A check for five thousand dollars that she'd never cashed? And she'd obviously earned it. Boy, how she'd earned it. Placing a hand on her abdomen, she wondered if the five grand included the overtime she'd unquestionably put in.

What would those Hollywood directors say about her acting abilities now? None of them could claim she hadn't gone all out to completely immerse herself in the role of Kyle's wife. Thing was, she'd probably immersed herself a bit too deep this time. Thinking about the possibility of your childhood pet getting hit by a car to help you cry on cue was one thing. But playing a wife and then actually getting pregnant was carrying her acting technique with the leading man way too far.

At some point she must have ventured from classical acting into improvisational theater.

Pulling a black purse from the dresser drawer, she unzipped the inside pocket and reached inside. Unless Kyle was some kind of Vegas magician who could make things appear through sleight of hand, he'd been telling the truth. Otherwise, how to explain a check from Kyle Williams made out to her in the amount of five thousand dollars?

There was no denying now that she'd entered into some kind of business deal with Kyle. Entered it and completed it, judging from the sizable check in her hand. But the baby wasn't part of the deal.

At the top of the stairs, she glanced down to where Kyle was sprawled on the sofa, rubbing his hands on the jeans that covered his obviously-muscled thighs. Was he nervous about something? He'd been acting like the king of the castle since he'd shown up at Leslie's door a few hours earlier. Maybe he had some acting skills of his own.

He looked up as she started down the stairs. Danielle held the purse in one hand and the check in the other.

"Found it." She triumphantly waved the check in the air. "I haven't used this purse since the accident. I didn't even know this check was in here. So, that's why it wasn't cashed."

"Probably just as well you didn't find it before I showed up. Without me being able to explain what it was for, you might have freaked out wondering how you got it."

"I'm still pretty freaked out, if you want to know the truth."

"About me, the baby, the money part of this thing—or all three?" Kyle's eyes bored into her.

"I admit I've always thought I'd eventually get married and have a baby. But it's pretty shocking to find out I'm well on the way to all that, and I literally do not have a clue about what happened. I mean, it looks like I just did it for some quick cash." She sagged onto the sofa next to Kyle.

He pulled her close to him. "Don't keep beating yourself up, Danielle. Yes, you needed some cash, and the promise of some fairly easy money was hard to resist. We were attracted to each other. And our wedding was a spur of the moment thing with a plan to annul it after the week was over."

Looking into his dark eyes, she could picture how a woman might be drawn into his spell. But her? And on a whim?

"You're not exactly making it sound like a classic love story, Kyle."

He pushed an errant lock of hair from her eyes, letting his hand linger on her cheek. "It didn't start out in a typical way, but I guarantee you that it turned into a love story. We did fall in love. And by the end of the week, we weren't so sure we wanted to sign any annulment papers."

Could she believe him?

Did she want to believe him?

"I-I just wish I could remember," she stammered.

Drawing her closer to his wide chest, he said, "I wish you could remember too. Because it's a beautiful memory."

His mouth was close enough to hers that she was sure he would kiss her. She couldn't control the acceleration of her breathing. Maybe if he kissed her like he did in Vegas—what? Did she expect all of her memories to come flooding back? Simply from a kiss?

Or maybe it would take more.

What was she thinking? Look what happened when she'd had sex with a stranger. A stranger she was married to, but still…

Kyle pulled away from her, appearing to think better of acting on his instinctual urge. "I have a proposal for you. Another sort of business deal."

Her heart jumped. What more could he have in mind? She wasn't doing such a great job with business deals. Getting pregnant, then not remembering to cash her paycheck—she'd probably be a lot better off if she refrained from any future business dealings with Kyle Williams.

"What kind of business deal?" she ventured.

"Continue our marriage—as a sort of marriage of convenience. At least until the baby is born."

"I don't get it." What kind of convenience was he talking about? The convenience for him of on-demand sex with her? She wasn't buying it.

"Look, I'll lay it out, plain and simple." He stood up and folded his arms across his chest. "You've been—excuse my language—sponging off your best friend Leslie for more than a month. You don't have a job. You're pregnant. With my baby."

She struggled to keep the indignation out of her voice. "What's your point?"

"So, you could use a place to stay. We're legally married. And I'll be starting a new job next week with full health insurance benefits."

"A new job?"

"Yeah, I accepted a position as General Manager of a big resort in Cottonwood Ridge. It's about a two-hour drive from here."

"What about the old job? The bonus, the promotion, and all that?"

He shifted from one foot to the other. "Yeah, well, I'm not working there anymore. I realized I didn't want to make a future at an organization that would expect me to shack up with a female co-worker to find out trade secrets."

She sniffed and wilted back into the sofa cushions. "That's very noble of you. But maybe I shouldn't make my future by shacking up with a man, so I can have a roof over my head and get my doctor's bills paid."

He sat beside her. "Let's get on the same page as far as what 'shacking-up' means. I'm not saying sex has to be part of the deal. Only if you want it to be."

"And I guess you're thinking that with our track record, you'll convince me to want sex to be part of the deal pretty quickly."

He grinned. "To be completely honest, I wouldn't mind that. But there are no strings attached. I got you into this…situation…and I want to make sure you're okay. And we're talking about *my* baby too. So, I want to make sure he or she gets the proper medical care."

"But it sounds kind of awkward. We scarcely know each other."

"Correction: we know each other very well." He winked at her. "You just don't remember it."

"I-I don't know…"

He gave her a heart-melting grin. "I'm telling you, you really do like me. And I'm not a bad guy."

Was this how he sucked her in the first time? That irresistible grin. Those dark eyes that beckoned her to…what? It wouldn't be that hard to stop resisting and go along with his idea. He'd awakened a sensation of arousal that must have emerged during their honeymoon.

She quickly pulled herself back to the present. Time to think rationally. She couldn't let her feelings control an important decision the way they must have when she'd first met Kyle.

He looked at her expectantly.

"I need to talk to my grandmother about this," she suddenly blurted out. "She's the only family member I have that I can trust. Could you drop me off at her apartment on your way to check into the hotel?"

"Sure thing," he said. Then he sent her one of those winks that turned her sensible thoughts to mush. "Any chance you'll join me at the hotel tonight?"

"Just because Dr. Chartoff said we were free to have sex doesn't give you carte blanche to pick up where you left off in Vegas."

"Well, you can't blame a guy for asking," Kyle said, flashing a mischievous grin.

Taking in his playful expression, she couldn't help feeling it wouldn't be long before he led her down a familiar path.

* * *

About five minutes later, Kyle and Danielle pulled up in front of the Ponderosa Manor Apartments, a complex of mid-rise buildings for active adults older than fifty-five.

"Look, there's Nana Rose coming down the street right now," Danielle said, spotting her grandmother on the sidewalk with several friends. "She's the one with the blue jogging suit."

"Retirement sure isn't what it used to be," Kyle said. "Doesn't look like any of these folks are spending their days in a rocking chair."

"Not around here. If it's too cold or snowy to take a run or brisk walk outdoors, they're on the treadmill in the gym or swimming laps in the indoor pool." Watching her grandmother chat with friends, she filled with admiration for the silver-haired woman who was barely seventy. "When Nana takes a break and sits down, she's either surfing the Web or making a schedule of volunteer activities for the residents at this complex."

"Cool." His face turned serious. "You were lucky to have a fine woman like that to finish raising you after your mom passed away."

Danielle quickly turned to Kyle. "How did you know—?" She stopped mid-question. It had become apparent that she had revealed more than a few things about herself to him during their one-week honeymoon. What more did he know about her? And what did she know about him? Or what had she known before that accident wiped out her memories of the week they spent together?

Danielle rolled down her window and waved as her grandmother approached the car. "Nana," she called out. "I'm so glad to see you."

The other woman's face beamed when she spotted Danielle. Nana hurried over to hug Danielle after she climbed out of the car, with Kyle sprinting around the front of the vehicle to her side.

Kyle cleared his throat, and it reminded Danielle of the purpose of the impromptu visit. She gestured toward him and said, "Nana Rose, this is my friend, Kyle. He's visiting here from…from—"

"I live in California, but I'm moving to Colorado for a new job," Kyle finished for her. "It's a pleasure to meet you. Danielle's told me so many good things about you."

Nana smiled and extended her hand to Kyle, her eyes sizing him up. "I could swear I hear a touch of Texas twang in your voice."

"You've got a good ear, ma'am. I grew up in the Austin area, but I've been living in Los Angeles the past few years."

"I grew up in Texas myself. Came here to Colorado as a young bride." Nana nodded, and her smile grew bigger. "My late husband wanted to live near the mountains. I've never regretted moving here, even though Texas is a heavenly place too."

"But you're not actually in the mountains," Kyle said.

"No, it's flat here, but we're only about an hour's drive east of Rocky Mountain National Park."

"This seems like a nice little town."

"It is," Nana agreed. "Only about ten thousand people here, so everyone knows most everybody else."

Kyle smiled. "Sounds perfect."

Danielle took in the exchange and felt perplexed. Why didn't she know that Nana Rose had grown up in Texas? And somehow Nana had told Kyle about her background within a few minutes of meeting him. What kind of spell did that man have over women?

"Nana, do you have a couple of minutes to talk to me? In your apartment, I mean." She wanted to make sure her grandmother realized she wanted a private conversation. Not a good idea to discuss a whirlwind marriage, honeymoon, and pregnancy right on the sidewalk.

"Of course, I do, dear." Nana put her arm around her. "I always have time for you."

"Glad I finally got to meet you, ma'am," Kyle said, heading back around to the driver side of his rental car. He turned to Danielle. "Should I pick you up after I check in at the hotel?"

"Um, I guess so." She hoped Nana hadn't gotten the wrong impression from Kyle's comment about checking in at the hotel. She certainly didn't want her grandmother to think she'd be sharing a hotel room with him. Then Danielle reminded herself that the story she was about to tell Nana would be equally juicy. Actually, even more so.

After they stepped out of the elevator, entered Nana's third-floor apartment, and settled at the dining table with cold glasses of lemonade, an uncomfortable silence sucked the air out of the room.

A moment passed, and then Nana said, "I suspect you want to talk to me about that young man I just met."

Propping her elbow on the table, Danielle rested her chin in her palm and nodded. How was she going to tell her grandmother about what she'd done in Las Vegas? Especially since she couldn't even remember any of it? It was almost like she was repeating a tale of gossip she'd heard.

"Was he your boyfriend while you were out in California?" Nana gently asked.

Danielle shook her head. "I didn't even have a boyfriend while I was out there. And even though Walter was my fiancé for almost two years, I told him he was free to see whoever he wanted before I left for California."

Nana snorted. "Puh-leeze. I don't know how you ever called that man your fiancé."

Ignoring Nana's impertinent remark about Walter, Danielle mumbled, "Well, he's sure not my fiancé anymore."

"What are you trying to tell me?"

"Oh, Nana." Danielle couldn't stop herself from sobbing. "I know you raised me better than this…"

"Spill it, girl."

When her grandmother's voice took on that no-nonsense tone, Danielle knew telling the truth was the only option. She had to tell Nana everything Kyle had told her from the time they'd met in a gas station parking lot in Barstow until he'd shown up at Leslie's door that morning.

When Danielle got to the part about the picture on Kyle's phone that showed them undressed in a hot tub, Nana gasped and said, "Oh…my." Then she sighed, made a clucking sound, and continued, "I don't know why young people always think their generation invented sex. How does everyone think they got here in the first place? Believe me, you can't tell me anything that's going to shock me. It's all been done before."

"I can't believe I did this, Nana." Danielle met her grandmother's eyes. "But unless Kyle is some big-time swindler, I'm married to him. And Dr. Chartoff confirmed I'm pregnant—exactly far enough along that it must have happened during that week I can't remember."

A slow smile formed on Nana's face. "It's not the first time a woman can't believe what she did with a good-looking man." She patted her granddaughter's hand. "And I don't expect it will be the last time."

"I don't know what to do. He wants me to come with him to his new job in Cottonwood Ridge. So he can make sure I'm taken care of until the baby's born."

"And after that?"

Danielle shrugged. “I guess that depends on whether I fall in love with him again.”

Nana looked at her with a knowing expression. “I have a funny feeling that won’t be too hard for you to do.”

“Nana, you only met him for a minute or two.”

Her grandmother laughed. “I’m a pretty good judge of character. You’ve done a lot better than you would have with that Ferguson fellow.”

“What are you saying?”

Nana patted Danielle’s cheek. “I’m saying you may have hit the jackpot in Vegas. I think you should go with your new husband and make sure my little great-grandchild is born big and healthy. By the time the baby arrives, you’ll know whether you want to stay with Kyle or not.”

Danielle couldn’t hide her shock. She wasn’t sure what she’d expected her grandmother to suggest. Consult an attorney? Tell Kyle he was on the hook for child support, but she’d take care of her own living arrangements, thank you very much?

“But I barely know him,” she protested. “What if he’s some serial killer?”

“You already spent a week with him, and he didn’t kill you.” Nana stroked Danielle’s shoulders. “You make your own decision, honey. All I’m saying is if it were me—well, I’d take a chance on him.”

“Nana, I’m seeing a side of you I never knew about.”

Her grandmother smiled, and then her face turned serious. “But if you go with him, I want you to send me a text message first thing every morning and at nine o'clock every night to let me know you're okay."

CHAPTER SIX

A little over a week later, Kyle couldn't wait to load the last of Danielle's belongings into his own SUV and begin their drive to Cottonwood Ridge. He still couldn't believe she'd agreed to accompany him to the town where he would begin his new job. Or that Nana Rose was onboard with the idea.

Now his wife's friend, Leslie, was a different story. As he stowed a box of Danielle's things in the back of his Explorer, he could make out Leslie's voice coming through her living room window.

"I'm telling you again that you are more than welcome to stay at my place as long as you need," Leslie said. "Even after the baby's born. You don't have to move in with that guy if you don't want to."

He breathed out a long sigh. Too bad Little Miss Sunshine hadn't been around to serve as a witness at the wedding chapel in Vegas. She sure would've added to the festivities.

Uh-uh. Not in this universe.

Bounding onto the porch and opening the front door, he felt like a guy showing up at a fancy restaurant without a shirt. Leslie's expression could easily have suited the maître d' in the most exclusive place in New York City when faced with a sloppily-dressed customer.

"All right then." He forced himself to smile at Leslie. "You two ladies said your good-byes and all that? We have a decent drive to Cottonwood Ridge, and Danielle wants to stop at Nana Rose's apartment before we hit the road."

He wanted to tell Leslie to keep her nose out of their business, but was that really fair? Deep down, he knew she was concerned about Danielle. And he couldn't deny that she was a good friend. Driving practically all the way to Utah to retrieve Danielle from the hospital after the accident. Then letting Danielle stay in her house for almost two months.

Besides, he had to give Leslie credit for being the first one to figure out that Danielle was pregnant. Then she was the one who got Danielle right into the doctor's office and made sure she did everything necessary to help ensure a healthy pregnancy. So, he'd ignore her remark about how Danielle didn't have to go with him.

Leslie clutched her friend, and Kyle couldn't help thinking it reminded him of a kid who didn't want to relinquish a favorite toy to let someone else take a turn. Whatever…he was sure Leslie truly had Danielle's best interests at heart.

Taking his wife by the hand, he guided her toward the door and gave Leslie a backward glance and sincere smile. "Thanks again for everything you've done for Danielle."

"Be careful," Leslie said to Danielle, her eyes showing a mixture of sadness and trepidation. "Call or text me when you arrive. You have that new cell phone, so be sure to use it."

"Will do." Danielle smiled and waved her new phone as if it were a trophy.

Crossing her arms across her chest, Leslie gave Kyle a wary expression and then turned to her friend. "I'm only a couple of hours away, so I can come right away if you need me."

"She'll be fine," Kyle said, leading Danielle to the porch. Then remembering how well Leslie had cared for his wife, he turned and added, "You're welcome to come for a visit. I'm sure Danielle would be happy to see you."

Was he imagining that both women simultaneously breathed what seemed like sighs of relief? He sure wasn't intending to break up their friendship. The only thing he wanted was to get his marriage off on the right track. Okay, so maybe the marriage had been stalled at the station for a few weeks, but now he was determined to get it back on track.

One more round of hugs, and then he got Danielle settled in his SUV, now filled with her belongings. Good thing he'd dropped off all of his things at their new two-bedroom apartment in Cottonwood Ridge on the way from Los Angeles. After more than a year living in a furnished apartment in L.A., he looked forward to a place with furniture that he actually owned.

He'd ordered a king-sized bed with a comfy

mattress for Danielle. And a double bed for the second bedroom. Just in case that's where she wanted him to sleep. He wasn't going to force himself on her. Sleeping arrangements—and whatever else happened after the lights went out—were all up to her. That's what he'd promised her when he'd proposed that they give their marriage another try.

Casting a sidelong glance at her in the passenger seat, he admired her profile and the cascade of golden hair covering her shoulders. Oh man, she might be two months pregnant, but she looked beyond hot. There was still no sign of a baby bump, and her t-shirt showed off her breasts. How was he going to keep his hands off of her when he got her alone in their apartment?

But he had to figure out a way. He knew she still didn't completely trust him because she couldn't remember how things had played out during their honeymoon week. She would fall in love with him again—there was no way he'd let her slip away this time. And the baby made it even more essential that he convince her how good they were together.

Kyle pulled away from Leslie's house. "You know, I was just thinking that a lot of the females working at that medical building where you saw the doctor look a lot like Leslie."

"What do you mean?"

"Well, almost every woman I saw had the same haircut. That pixie thing—they all had it going on."

"Actually, that was Leslie's doing."

"She controls the nurses' hairstyles on top of

everything else?"

"One of the nurses in the Emergency Department was treated for breast cancer this year. When she came back to work, her hair was just starting to grow in after the chemo."

"I don't get the connection," he said.

"Leslie organized a lot of the nurses to cut their hair short in support of their colleague whose hair had fallen out. When I left town for California, Leslie's hair was practically a buzz cut."

"So, that's why I didn't recognize her when she came back to her house that first day. The picture you showed me in Vegas was of the two of you horseback riding, and she had a long ponytail."

"Yeah, it's going to take a while for that to grow back."

"Nice of her to do that," Kyle said. Damn nice, in fact. His initial impression of Leslie had done a one-eighty as he'd gotten to know her better.

He turned the SUV onto the street where Danielle's grandmother lived. "Does Nana Rose know we're coming over to say good-bye?"

Danielle nodded. "She said she'll wait for us."

They found her sitting on a bench among neatly-trimmed bushes in front of her apartment building. She looked like she was enjoying the autumn sunshine. "There you are," Nana called out when Danielle emerged from the car. "Come on upstairs. I have something for you before you go."

Kyle followed the two women into the elevator and then into Nana's apartment. They both politely turned down Nana's offer of a cold beverage.

He felt awkward, as though he were a crasher

at a family event. When Nana handed a gift-wrapped box to Danielle, he wondered whether he was intruding on their privacy. Wait—he was part of the family now, wasn't he? Maybe legally, but he knew it would take time to build a solid relationship. Still, Danielle was worth the time and effort that would take.

Danielle's eyes welled with tears when she pulled off the wrapping paper to reveal a framed photograph. "Oh, Nana…I'll treasure this. Thank you so much."

He could make out an inscription at the bottom of the frame that read: *Mothers and grandmothers are special friends.*

Holding the frame so Kyle could see it better, Danielle said, "That's my mother with Nana and me when I was…what? About five or six years old, Nana?"

She nodded at Danielle, and Kyle saw Nana's eyes misting up as well.

"I'd say that's about right." Nana's face brightened. "I thought you might like a memory of us with you in your new home."

Danielle hugged her grandmother. "That's so sweet. But you'll come visit us, won't you? Especially after the baby is born."

Kyle's eyes met Nana's. Was he imagining things again, or were both he and Nana Rose thinking the same thing? Was Danielle implying that she'd still be with him after the baby was born? Then again, maybe he'd read too much into her remark. After all, he'd proposed that they live together until the baby arrived, so he could take care of her during the pregnancy.

And try to get their marriage going again.

She sure wasn't going to give birth and then take off the next day, was she? No, she'd definitely stick around for at least a few weeks. Of course, he fully intended to make her never want to leave him again.

Nana chuckled. "You know you'll have a hard time keeping me away from my great-grandchild."

"You're welcome to visit any time, ma'am," Kyle said. They shared a smile, and it felt like a good sign. He'd gotten off on a good foot with Danielle's grandmother. "I think we'd better get on the road now. I'm sure Danielle is anxious to settle in at our new home."

"Now, you take your time driving," Nana admonished. "No need to rush. Safety first."

Pulling out his car keys, Kyle said, "You won't catch me exceeding any speed limits in this town. Some cop pulled me over last week when I was returning to the hotel. Said my license plate was hanging crooked."

"Really?" Nana asked.

"Seriously, he checked me out like I was on the Most Wanted List before he let me drive away." Kyle frowned. "I guess they either don't like strangers around here, or it was a slow day in town, crime-wise."

Nana looked at him with a strange expression. "Maybe so."

* * *

By the time they pulled off the highway at the

Cottonwood Ridge exit a few hours later, Danielle couldn't decide whether apprehension or excitement was winning the battle of her emotions. Each time excitement took the lead, apprehension would bubble up and surge a little bit ahead.

Was this the beginning of a fantastic new life with a husband and baby? Or maybe it was a temporary charade that would end up with her as a single mom. Thoughts of her mother's struggles with keeping a roof over their heads suddenly came to the forefront. And how hard her mother had tried to make sure Danielle would have an easier time of things.

She guessed there were some things you couldn't protect your kids from, no matter how hard you tried. Or warn them about. Like a car breakdown followed by a ride with a handsome stranger, and then…no, her mother never could have predicted a half-fake, half-real marriage in Vegas and a baby on the way as the result.

Nothing fake about the pregnancy. Dr. Chartoff had confirmed that.

But what about the marriage? Real or fake?

I guess that's what we're going to find out starting tonight.

Kyle's voice interrupted her thoughts. "What did Walter say when you told him you were leaving town again?"

"He seemed surprised." It would probably be more accurate to say he'd been pissed. Also accurate to say that even though she'd most likely burned that bridge when she'd told Walter he could date whoever he wanted when she left for

California, she'd definitely exploded any remaining bridge supports when she told him she was moving to Cottonwood Ridge with Kyle. She'd left out most of the details, such as the Vegas marriage and resulting pregnancy. As far as she was concerned, it wasn't necessary to spread her personal business all over New Loudon right now.

Kyle chuckled. "I'll bet he was surprised, to say the least. The guy didn't know a good thing when he had it."

Danielle couldn't help feeling a flash of pleasure when Kyle referred to her as a good thing. "Let's not talk about Walter anymore. He's ancient history. We broke up—if there was anything to even break up—when I moved to California."

"That's what you told me in Vegas." He checked the rearview mirror and then focused his glance straight ahead. "But I wanted to double-check that he's not trying to heat things up again."

"There's nothing to heat up," Danielle said. "Forget about him."

"Works for me."

"It's pretty here," she said, taking in the mountains that provided a storybook backdrop to the town. She wouldn't be doing any skiing down those mountains this winter. By the time the trails were covered with snow, her pregnancy would be showing. And her center of gravity would be off-kilter.

No, she undeniably wouldn't be taking any chances hitting the slopes this season.

She caught Kyle quickly glancing at her as he pulled onto the main street of town. "I thought you'd like it," he said. "Even though I've only been here twice, I'm already falling in love with the place. It's a resort town, but there's a substantial year-round community too."

"And you were able to find us a two-bedroom apartment?" There, she'd said it. Find *us* an apartment. It was a place for both of them. Not *his* apartment, but their home.

At least until the baby was born.

"Two bedrooms, two bathrooms, updated kitchen…I think you're gonna like it."

"Planning ahead for a second bedroom to use as the nursery?" He sure was giving her plenty of time to decorate the nursery for the baby. But how long would she and the baby be living with Kyle after the birth? That was still to be determined.

He cleared his throat. "Actually, I figured I'd give you some space. I already told you that you could have your own bedroom if you wanted to try and make a go of our marriage. You're not obligated to get intimate with me. This is all about making sure you have a healthy pregnancy."

"Thank you." She didn't know what else to do but thank him. For his generosity, of course. As far as his promise of not necessarily getting intimate…well, she should probably be thankful for that too.

Or should she be thankful? She must have enjoyed what they'd done to create their growing child. If only she could remember exactly how she'd felt.

But did it matter how she'd felt before? Or whether he'd acted like he truly cared about her?

Anyway, he must have. Look at him now. He'd promised to cover all her expenses through childbirth, pretty much with no strings attached.

He claimed he wasn't expecting anything from her beyond a platonic relationship. And yet…

I think I could warm up to something more than a platonic relationship with him.

"I really appreciate you stepping up to the plate to help me with medical expenses." She squeezed his forearm, struggling to keep her emerging feelings below the surface. "And everything else."

"Yeah, I've been falsely accused of not always finishing things that I've started once or twice. No worries—I'm following this through to the finish line."

She pulled her hand away from his forearm. "Define *finish line.*"

Kyle eased his vehicle into a parking space in front of an apartment building. Turning to Danielle, he winked. "I think you're the one who gets to come up with that definition, darlin'."

* * *

After unlocking and opening the door to the apartment, Kyle stepped back and swept out his arm, beckoning Danielle to enter first. "Hold on a minute," he said, suddenly blocking the doorway. "I know that very little about the story of us has been traditional so far. How about if I mix things up and follow the customary practice of carrying my bride across the threshold of our home?"

She blushed. "Kyle, there's no need—"

"I didn't say it's mandatory," he cut in. "It's

something I want to do."

She laughed. "To prove you're strong enough to lift me?"

He snorted. "Hell, I can bench press more than you weigh without breaking a sweat."

"I guess I should take that as a compliment."

"I guess you should." He grinned with amusement. "I don't know whether carrying the bride across the threshold is a custom that's supposed to ward off evil spirits, prevent you from tripping on the doorway, or give the impression that you're not so eager to consummate our marriage."

"Well, that's already been taken care of." She smirked. "The last one, I mean."

Winking, he said, "But the neighbors don't have to know about that. Come on, Mrs. Williams, I'm carrying you into our home."

He gathered her into his arms, and his mind immediately went back to the day he'd tracked her down to Leslie's house. He'd caught Danielle when she fainted after he announced himself as her husband. Yet here she was, only about a week later, moving in with him. And as he held her in his arms this time, she was fully conscious and willing to be here.

He admitted that she hadn't exactly been at the high point of her life when she'd made that decision. Her old teaching job at the high school had already been filled. Maybe the promise of paid medical care was a big part of the reason she'd been willing to move in with him now.

But he didn't believe that was the only thing that had prompted Danielle to agree to his proposal.

He'd be on the hook to help pay for pregnancy expenses and child support anyway. She could have gone to court and sued to force him to meet his financial obligations.

But she hadn't.

And man, she sure smelled good. With her right up against him, he breathed in the scent of her perfume. Dropping his face, he nuzzled her hair. Danielle turned her head to the side and parted her lips slightly. What the—that definitely looked like a signal that she wanted him to kiss her.

Closing his eyes, he met her lips. Warm and delicious, exactly the way he remembered. When he eventually pulled away, he said, "That was really nice. I hope you didn't mind."

"It's a tradition, isn't it?" She raised her brows. "Everything will look on the up-and-up to any snoopy neighbors who might be peeking out their windows right now."

Was that what this was all about? Putting on a show for the neighbors? He'd been thinking that Danielle was softening toward him, but he'd momentarily forgotten about her being an actress. Just like she'd agreed before to act like his wife for a week so she could earn five grand, maybe now she was agreeing to keep up the masquerade a few months longer so her medical bills would be paid. Easier than hiring an attorney and filing a lawsuit, he supposed.

Maybe, maybe not. No matter what her motive, he was determined to make her fall in love with him again. She hadn't been play-acting for that entire week in Vegas. Nothing could convince him otherwise.

Even if she were only acting now, he'd make sure the acting turned to real-life. He'd done it before, and he'd do it again. No problem, right?

"I wasn't all that worried about nosy neighbors, but I'm glad to kiss you if that's what it takes to put their minds at rest," Kyle said.

"Mission accomplished."

She shifted in his arms, which Kyle took as a signal that she wanted him to put her down. Easing her back down to the floor inside the doorway, he said, "I'll bring the luggage inside later. Let me show you around the apartment."

He took her by the hand and guided her into the living room.

Looking around, she said, "Something seems to be missing. Like the furniture."

"Right. I figured you'd want to pick out the sofa, chairs, and whatever else we need. You probably have better decorating taste than I do anyway."

"Doesn't it take a long time to get furniture delivered?"

"There's a furniture store downtown. They have a warehouse out by the interstate, and they promise to deliver the day after we buy our furniture."

"Pretty convenient, but where do we sleep in the meantime?"

"I already took care of that." He steered her down the hallway and into the master bedroom. "I got this king-sized bed for you. I hope the white comforter will be okay for you for now. You can pick out whatever quilt or bedspread you'd like."

"That's sweet of you. And I could use a night table for that framed photo that Nana gave me. But that giant bed is all for me?"

Kyle nodded and grinned. "Unless you want me in there with you to keep you warm. And you're under no obligation."

"And you will be sleeping…where?"

He led her to the second bedroom. "There's a perfectly fine double bed in here that I can use. Like I said before, this will be okay with me. As long as that's where you want me to sleep."

Danielle turned to face him. "Sounds fair."

Did it? He supposed it was reasonable that a woman who couldn't even remember she was married to him would want to sleep in her own bed. But for how long?

In the meantime, he'd be a gentleman and wait until she felt comfortable enough to welcome him into her bed.

But he didn't want to wait *too* long.

There she was, filling out her jeans perfectly. And she probably didn't even realize the effect she was having on him with that snug t-shirt.

How long would it be until he'd see her unclothed again? He wasn't sure how much longer he could wait to make sweet love with her once more.

CHAPTER SEVEN

By the end of the next week, Danielle couldn't deny that she and Kyle had fallen into a pleasant routine. He had settled in nicely as the new manager at the resort. She felt good about living in the town of Cottonwood Ridge. It had been fun following Kyle's suggestion to select whatever furnishings she liked for their apartment. The place looked downright homey.

And they were still sleeping in separate bedrooms.

Danielle wasn't sure if it was the stress of starting a challenging new job that kept Kyle from doing more than pretty much exchanging pleasantries when he got home from work. He was working more than a standard eight-hour workday, making sure things were under control and preparations underway for the upcoming ski season.

She couldn't complain that he wasn't acting concerned about her well-being. Quite the opposite.

If she wasn't up and about when he left for work, he'd text her a little later to make sure she was okay. And he checked in again a couple of times during the day. As soon as he got home from work, he'd ask what he could do to make her comfortable.

Maybe it was the crisp mountain air or perhaps the fact that that she was moving toward the second trimester of her pregnancy that caused a change. Whatever it was, Danielle had gotten her energy back and felt much better overall. Now that her queasiness had disappeared, she enjoyed preparing a nice dinner for Kyle each evening.

"You don't have to go to all this trouble for me," he said when he got home from work on Friday night. "I don't want you on your feet too much or straining to lift heavy things."

She laughed. "Kyle, I'm fine. Dr. Chartoff said so." Her face darkened for an instant. "At least pregnancy-wise. Now, my memory is another matter. But I can certainly pick up a small skillet and stand here cooking for half an hour."

"But I'm supposed to be taking care of you. You're not here to wait on me."

"Well, I have to eat too." She shrugged.

"Was that a play on words about *eating for two?*"

"Actually, no." Danielle rolled her eyes. "The reality of a changing body image isn't the easiest adjustment."

"All I can say is you look fantastic in that long top—what do you call it?"

"A tunic."

"Oh yeah." Kyle cringed. "I should've known

that. Anyway, I like the color, and it has—what do they call it? A slimming effect."

"Listen to you, Mr. Fashion Expert." Danielle smirked and let out a huff.

After she waved off his offer of help with finishing up dinner preparation, Kyle promised to be back as soon as he changed out of his business clothes. A few minutes later, they settled at the dining table where Danielle had placed a platter of sautéed chicken seasoned with rosemary.

Sitting across from him, she couldn't help admiring his broad shoulders and the square set of his jaw.

Did she have an interest in modifying their sleeping arrangements? Snuggling up at night with the handsome man now obviously enjoying the food she'd prepared? Maybe allowing nature to take its course and turn snuggling into something even more intimate?

Probably definitely.

But as strong as her physical attraction to Kyle was, she couldn't dismiss that troubling sensation in her gut that told her she wanted to know him better before considering more than snuggling with him. Even though what they'd done in Vegas had transformed her into a mother-to-be.

But it was time to focus on what is, right now. And right now, a friendly, good-looking man who happened to be her husband and the father of her child was sitting about three feet from her. In their home. And he'd promised that she and the baby would be taken care of right through the delivery.

She needed to find out more about what made

him tick. More details about his personal background and how he'd eventually ended up in that parking lot with her in Barstow, California. They were going to be spending at least the next few months living together. If he knew private things about her, she deserved to learn more about him too.

Deciding to proceed cautiously with breaking the ice, she said, "I'm glad you're enjoying the chicken. Did I happen to tell you that I knew how to cook before you married me, or were you willing to take a chance on eating burned food every night going forward?"

"To be honest," he replied, pausing to take a sip of water and then lean back in his chair, "we didn't quite get around to picking out a china pattern and all those good kind of activities before we got hitched." A smile slowly lit up his face. "And I doubt either of us thought ahead to what we'd be having for dinner after our honeymoon week."

"Right." She nodded. "The marriage was only supposed to last a week anyway. So, why would you care about my cooking skills?"

"It's just a bonus, darlin'. I love you either way—whether you're a master chef or someone who can't even boil water."

Did he say that he loved her?

The words *I love you* had undeniably been said. But there was no sense getting too worked up about it. He'd probably meant it the same way someone would say they loved pizza or a favorite TV show. A description of something enjoyable. Not everlasting, can't-live-without-you feelings.

"But I must have told you a few things about my background," she continued. "When you first came to New Loudon, you already knew about my old boyfriend, Walter. You knew about my mother and grandmother too. And I really don't know anything about your past."

"What's your point?"

Taking a deep breath, she plunged in. "I know it's not the kind of thing couples should dwell on, but I can't help wondering why you hadn't already settled down and gotten married. I mean, a lot of guys start thinking about marriage by the time they hit thirty."

He sat up straight and looked at her directly. "I've thought about marriage. I was briefly engaged to a woman I knew in college. But she broke it off."

"Do you mind if I ask why?"

"She didn't like my financial status. Thought she could do better. She's actually married to one of my college buddies now." His mouth formed a taut line and his nostrils flared as he took a deep breath. "Make that a former buddy. We're not exactly tight these days."

"Oh, I'm sorry," Danielle said automatically, the way most people do when someone relates any kind of bad news. At his startled look, she realized that maybe she shouldn't have said she was sorry an old girlfriend had broken up with him and married his friend.

"You think I should get friendly with both of them again?" Kyle cocked his head to the side.

"I didn't exactly mean that," she said. Sure, it must have hurt him at the time. But *she* was married to Kyle now. She was glad that he was still available when their paths crossed, wasn't she? "Or maybe what I'm sorry about is that your friendship with your old buddy got wrecked. But I'm not sorry that you were single when we met."

"I guess that's a start in the right direction," Kyle said. "For us trying to be a couple, that is."

She fought off the urge to ask him what being a couple meant to him. Because she didn't want it to be entirely about having sex.

But would making love with Kyle be wrong? A tantalizing sensation whooshed through her. She could tell he was attracted to her. And the feeling had become oh-so mutual. He was totally gorgeous. And there was no denying that he treated her excellently.

She imagined them ignoring the dinner she'd prepared and making their way to the master bedroom. Kyle could make her feel incredible, couldn't he? If only she could remember the details about when they'd made love before.

A little voice inside her suddenly told her that she should stop doing things in the wrong order.

Get to know him first, the annoying voice said.

Then Danielle smiled at Kyle and heard herself say, "Right, we need to work on that coupling thing. Get that down pat before we're immersed in parenthood."

He returned her smile. "Coupling—I like the sound of that."

"Actually, I meant that in the sense of getting to know each other better first. Not immediately jumping into the physical part."

"Gotcha." His shoulders slumped enough for Danielle to take note. He quickly straightened, and his face brightened. "I also like the way you said we shouldn't *immediately* get physical again. And that's okay. Maybe it'll happen down the road, but I'll leave that up to you."

"I appreciate that." She didn't mind leaving open the possibility that they'd eventually be intimate again. But she wanted to take her time. Even with him radiating manliness from every pore, she didn't intend to mindlessly jump into bed with him. Maybe she'd done that when they first met, but now she was going to act more responsibly.

Leaning back in his chair again with his arms spread out on the armrests, he was the picture of self-assured masculinity. "What do you want to know about me? Because I already know quite a bit about you from the week we spent together." He winked. "Go ahead and fire away with your questions. I'm an open book."

She thought for a moment. Exactly what did she already know about Kyle? He'd been living in Los Angeles when they met in that parking lot. At the time, he worked for some resort company that thought pairing up employees to pose as honeymoon couples was a good way to improve business operations. His cash flow was good enough that he could afford to pay five thousand dollars to a stranger for help in completing a job assignment.

Yet a former fiancée had dumped him for a guy with better financial prospects. And Kyle had ended up deciding he didn't like the way his employer did things, so he'd found this new job as the manager of a ski resort in Cottonwood Ridge.

Oh yeah, and he'd grown up around Austin, Texas. Nana Rose had gotten that information out of him within moments of meeting him.

Danielle considered her new husband with a blend of anticipation and anxiety. "Who *are* you, Kyle?"

"Kyle Williams. Age 31. Texas transplant. Overall good guy and hardcore football fan," he said as he stood to clear the dinner plates from the table. He shot her one of his disarming smiles. "I've got my driver's license in my wallet, if that's what you need. Photo ID and all."

Was there no end to this man's ability to conjure up official government documents? He'd produced a marriage certificate. Now he wanted her to check out his driver's license. What if he were some kind of counterfeiter or con artist or career criminal?

She'd been influenced by Nana to trust Kyle and move in with him until the baby was born. Nana always seemed to have good judgment. But what if her grandmother had given her bad advice this time?

If only she'd lingered in Las Vegas five minutes longer before saying good-bye to Kyle and setting out for Colorado. Then she wouldn't have been in the path of that car that had plowed head-on into her. She wouldn't even have gotten to that spot on the highway yet.

If she'd started her journey five or ten minutes later, her memory of the week with Kyle wouldn't have disappeared. She would remember everything that had happened from the moment they'd met in that parking lot. She would remember why she'd thought spending a week with a stranger was a good idea. She would remember what had prompted her to actually recite wedding vows and marry him.

She would remember how he'd made her feel when they made love.

* * *

Since Danielle was asking about his background, Kyle figured it was a good time to provide her with his recent test results. She'd probably be interested in what the lab reported. And if she wasn't interested…well, she should be.

He returned to the dining table a couple of minutes later, with his wallet in one hand and an envelope in the other. Placing his driver's license on the table, he said, "By the way, I'll be trading in my California license for a Colorado ID. I'm intending to stay here."

She examined the driver's license, scrutinizing the front and then the back. "Looks like you really are Kyle Williams. But I wasn't so concerned whether that's your real name. I was thinking more about your background, your family, that kind of thing."

"Makes sense," he said, tucking his ID back into his wallet. "I shared quite a bit of those details with you during our honeymoon, but I'm happy to give you the full rundown again."

"Damn amnesia," she muttered.

"We'll get through it, baby." His large hand

covered hers. "We'll make new memories. Good memories."

Danielle's face showed a hint of a smile, and she nodded.

"So, to get back to your fact-finding mission..." he drawled, "should I give you the story of my life, or do you want to shoot questions at me?"

He'd been trying to come across as a regular guy since he'd located Danielle at her friend's home in New Loudon. And in most ways, that's what he was.

But there was more to his background.

"I did tell you on our honeymoon about my parents' business and my decision to strike out on my own," he continued. The thing was, during their initial conversations, he'd kind of glossed over some of the specifics about what his parents did for a living. He'd seen before how it could complicate things. He'd seen it up close and personal when it affected his relationship with his former fiancée.

Because of his previous experience, he didn't want to give Danielle all the details until he was sure she loved him for who he really was.

Of course, thanks to that car accident, now she didn't even love him anymore. Not because he'd done anything to make her feel differently. She just couldn't remember falling in love with him.

Now that he thought about it, maybe he should give her the condensed version of his life story—leaving out the specifics of how wealthy his parents were—so he'd have more control over how the details flowed.

Before he could launch into his story, she made it even easier for him. “Why don’t you tell me what you think is important for me to know? Then I’ll follow up with any questions I can think of.”

“Perfect.” He tried to remember exactly how he’d initially described the chain of steakhouses his parents owned when he’d given Danielle his family history during their honeymoon.

Restaurant owners.

That’s how he’d described them. And when Danielle had asked what kind of restaurant they owned, he’d simply replied, “Steaks. Western-style.” That wasn’t lying, was it? Maybe it had given her the impression that his parents owned a single steakhouse, rather than a chain with almost three hundred locations.

Could he help it if he wasn’t good with details?

“You already know from when I spoke to your Nana Rose that I grew up in the Austin, Texas area,” he began. He compressed the story of his childhood into about thirty seconds, added another fifteen seconds to describe the lovable Golden Retriever he’d had as a kid, mentioned studying business in college, and gave a speedy overview of the two jobs he’d had before joining the company that sent him to Vegas on the undercover mission where he’d connected with Danielle. “Oh yeah, and my older sister is a doctor, and my parents are restaurant owners.”

“Restaurant owners.” She arched an eyebrow. “What kind of restaurant?”

“Steaks. Western-style.” He felt a sense of déjà vu about how the conversation was going. “I know you're not a vegetarian, so you're okay with that, right?"

"No problem at all. What kind of doctor is your sister?"

"She's one of the best pediatricians in Dallas. She's super-crazy about kids." His eyes went to Danielle's abdomen. "Knowing Samantha Jane, she'll have plenty of advice for us when the baby is born. Stereotypical big sister who knows more about everything than I do. Oh, and she dropped the middle name and started going by Samantha the day she left home for college."

"Does she know that we're having a baby?"

He shook his head. "That's the one thing I know more about at this point than she does."

"When were you planning to let your family know that you're going to be a daddy?"

He took a deep breath and yanked at his collar. "My parents don't even know I'm married yet. I was kind of waiting to find out whether we were going to make it permanent before I sprung it on them that I eloped in Vegas."

Danielle's eyes flashed, and astonishment swept over her face. "With me being in the third month of pregnancy? With their grandchild?" She let out a long exhale. "What if it takes me a few months to be sure of my decision? Or I'm not sure until after the baby's born? You're not going to tell them about us?"

"Whoa, hold on." He didn't want her to think that he was reluctant to let his parents know about *her*. Truth be told, he wanted nothing more than to tell his family—and everyone else he knew—that he had finally found the woman he wanted to make a life with. Happily ever after, and everything that went with it. "Up until barely two weeks ago, I had no idea whether you wanted to annul our marriage or not. Maybe I was wrong, but if we wiped the slate clean, I wasn't intending to tell my folks about our little…adventure…you know, what happened in Vegas. And I didn't know that we were going to have a baby."

Danielle's expression softened, and Kyle was able to exhale. Funny, he hadn't even realized he'd been holding his breath. It was a gut reaction while he waited to see if she'd been offended by what he said about not yet informing his parents.

"Whether we stay married or not, this baby is still their grandchild," she said. "They have a right to know about it."

"Agreed." He hoped his parents would take the news as well as Nana Rose had. "We'll have to put our heads together to figure out the best way to give them the news."

"I'll give it some thought." Danielle pointed to where he'd placed the envelope he'd brought from the bedroom. "So, what's in that envelope? Don't tell me you already composed a letter to your parents? *Dear Mom and Dad, I met a great girl in Vegas, we got married, and we'll be making you grandparents next May…"*

Kyle let out a snort. "Hell, no. You'd hear them hollering all the way from Texas if they opened a letter like that. I mean, they'd probably turn cartwheels over the baby. But my mom would carry on because she wasn't there for her son's wedding."

"I think we'll have to figure out a real creative way to break the news to them about us."

"Some major-league brainstorming is definitely going to be required."

"And you still haven't told me what's in the envelope."

Picking up the envelope, he stared at it for a few seconds. As though the right way to discuss the contents would be printed on the outside. A step-by-step guide to discussing the potential for sexually-transmitted diseases.

"Look, this isn't the easiest thing to say, but…well…I mean it's pretty obvious that we had sex without using a condom."

Danielle placed a hand on her abdomen. "Sure seems that way."

"Anyway, I got some lab work done last week." He handed her the envelope. "I wanted you to feel confident that I didn't give you something else in addition to our baby."

"Should I be concerned?"

"I passed with flying colors." He couldn't help giving her a smirk.

"Were you concerned that you might have picked up something from me?"

Shaking his head, he said, "You told me that you hadn't been with anyone for quite a while. Even though you claimed to have been engaged at some point to your friend, Walter."

"I still can't believe I told you something that personal when I'd only just met you."

"You did things that were a lot more personal than that." Kyle's expression turned even bolder. "If you catch my drift."

He couldn't help it. Thoughts of making love to her shot through his brain. A couple of months ago, they'd both been searching for something, someone, anything to make them feel wanted. And their sparks of attraction had quickly caught fire.

Once they'd agreed to pretend to be married for a week—and bolster their story with an authentic marriage certificate—their natural attraction to each other had grown along with the ease with which they interacted.

It hadn't taken much time at all before Danielle had let him completely undress her and ease her into the hot tub once they were in their honeymoon suite.

How could she forget the deep kisses they'd shared? The touching. The exploring. And then toweling off and moving to the bed.

Her voice interrupted his daydream. "Now I'm officially embarrassed," she said. "I feel like I did something I never did before—or at least in a way I never did it before—but I know nothing about it. You're the only one with the memory of it."

"I remember you told me it had never been that good for you before."

She looked at him skeptically. "Did I really say that, Kyle?"

"You did. And you can have it that good again, darlin'. All you have to do is say the word."

* * *

Just say the word.

Did she want to say the word? If she simply

nodded and uttered the word yes, she knew Kyle could have her in that king-sized bed in a matter of seconds. Touching her in places she hadn't been touched in a very long time.

That wasn't exactly true. She'd obviously been touched in those intimate places within the past three months. Otherwise, there'd be no baby growing inside of her. She just couldn't remember anything about it.

"Er…Kyle, how many times did I say the word during our honeymoon?"

There was his irresistible grin again. "At least every day."

"At least?" What had possessed her?

"We were married, Danielle. It was all legal. Everything was on the up-and-up."

"But it was a sham. You said we were going to get the marriage annulled at the end of the week. After you gathered your intelligence, and I got paid for helping you."

"I admit it started that way. But things changed."

"Because we had sex?"

"Maybe that was part of it."

"How big a part?" Danielle asked.

"Look, the sex wasn't everything." Kyle shook his head. "All I know is that we had one hell of a…well, I don't know exactly what. But by the end of the week, I didn't want to let whatever it was slip away."

"And I wasn't sure?"

"You said you hadn't been home in six months, and you needed to think about it. To talk to your grandmother. To figure out what the situation was with your old teaching job. To take a little time to be sure you weren't running in the wrong direction."

That sounded more like her. She'd never been one to make rash decisions. Although it sounded like she'd made an extremely rash decision when she'd gotten in the vehicle with Kyle in Barstow and then agreed to spend a week pretending to be his wife.

What had Kyle said about her running in the wrong direction? There was something about the word running that set off a strange sensation in her brain. A tiny drop of liquid slid off some kind of mental ice cube and wormed its way through her consciousness.

The last thing she remembered before waking up in that ambulance was getting into her car in Los Angeles and setting out for home. But now she remembered a thought she'd had as she made her way to the highway that headed toward Las Vegas and eventually to Colorado.

She'd felt like she was running. But she hadn't been sure if she was running away from a failed six-month adventure or running toward familiarity and security. Funny how your mind could put whatever spin it wanted on any situation.

She'd run away from the adventure of professional acting when it hadn't worked out. And run right into a new adventure, acting like a stranger's wife. Was adventure what she truly craved?

Or had she merely gotten sidetracked while

running back to the supposed security of a platonic relationship with Walter Ferguson and the familiarity of her hometown?

When would that mental ice cube finish melting and release her memories of what she'd been thinking when she'd agreed to Kyle's scheme?

CHAPTER EIGHT

"I'm sensing that you still need more time to figure out how this is all going to play out." Kyle said it as gently as possible, not wanting to let his disappointment show.

Did he want to hold her and kiss her and prove how he could satisfy her? Did he want to be her husband, her partner in life, her best friend?

He wanted all of it.

And he was pretty sure she wanted all of it too. If only she could remember what they'd experienced during that magical week. That dream week.

If the doctor hadn't confirmed Danielle's pregnancy, he could almost believe that it had all been a dream. Otherwise, he'd wonder if he'd conjured up the whole thing in his head. Maybe he had actually turned his Explorer around and headed back to L.A. after his female colleague had notified him that she'd bailed on their undercover mission.

But he knew that he hadn't turned the SUV around.

No way could he dream up something like what actually happened. If he could, he'd be a big-time Hollywood screenwriter, sitting around some fancy swimming pool making a deal for the next blockbuster.

Before he could think further about his mental status, Danielle's hand was on his. "Can you be patient with me a little longer?" she asked. "What we shared that week sounds more than special."

"It was," he said.

"I admit that I've known about the baby and what I must have done in Vegas for almost three weeks now. But it's hard to process all of it when everything that happened is like a big black hole in my memory. I want to remember it." She threw her hands up in the air. "I just can't."

Disappointment surged through him. He ached to experience once again what he'd felt in Vegas. To see all of her again—every inch of silky skin under that long thing she called a tunic and the jeans she had on. To press his own skin against hers and then make that ultimate connection.

It would happen again, wouldn't it? Maybe not tonight, but he knew they would become one again. He was still the same man she'd met just a few months before. She'd fallen in love with him then. It was just a matter of time before she fell in love with him again.

"I understand," he said, trying to keep the frustration out of his voice. "I told you there was no pressure if you wanted to live with me during your pregnancy. I'm leaving everything up to you."

"You're being very generous, Kyle."

"Not really. I think I have an obligation to make sure the mother of my child is taken care of while she's expecting."

A trace of regret showed in her face. "I hope I'm more than a mere obligation."

"Oh, you're much more than an obligation. I wish I could convince you of that."

Why didn't she realize what she meant to him? She was more than some responsibility he needed to fulfill. She was more than an object of sexual desire. She was that missing part he'd been looking for since he couldn't remember when.

As long as she loved him the same way. Just for who he was. Whether his parents were millionaires many times over or whether they were struggling to keep a single restaurant afloat. He had to be sure she'd stick with him no matter what his finances were.

The thought suddenly entered his head that he wasn't even sure that she loved him at all. Her growing love for him had all been whisked away by a run-in with a careening car and a blow to the head.

Could he bring back the magic of their initial week and stir those feelings within her again?

He was sure as hell going to try.

But not tonight. He'd told her that it was all up to her. And as much as he wanted to take the lead and whisk her into his arms, he'd let her call the shots.

Danielle's eyes turned wistful. "I wish you didn't have to convince me of anything. I wish I could just remember when we were together before."

"I wish that too." If she remembered their time together, he was sure they'd be heading to the bedroom right then.

Leaning over, he planted a chaste kiss on her cheek. "Thank you for this delicious dinner. Now let me return the favor and clean up everything in the kitchen."

"You don't have to do that," she protested.

"I *want* to do it." He smiled. "C'mon now, scoot. Relax, watch TV, go to bed early—whatever you need. Healthy mama, healthy baby. That's what we're shooting for."

It was true, he wanted to be sure that both Danielle and their baby were healthy. But he wanted more. Love, physical intimacy, and her promise to stand by him for better or for worse.

And he was determined to have it all.

* * *

The next morning, Danielle awoke in a tangle of covers. Had she invited Kyle into her bed? Turning on her side, she noted the pillow beside her perfectly fluffed exactly as when she'd gone to bed. She buried her nose in it and inhaled the faint scent of fabric softener.

No trace of a manly aroma to indicate that Kyle had been in her bed last night. But the state of the bed sheets pointed to some kind of activity taking place after she'd fallen asleep. What had she dreamed about? Maybe she had tried to recreate a love scene with Kyle from their honeymoon.

Perhaps the memory of their lovemaking was deep in her subconscious. Somewhere in the cells of her brain there could be a trail of thoughts and sensations—images of two bodies intertwined. Kissing, fondling, and then finally joining in rhythm as one.

Her heart rate ticked up a notch. She had to stop thinking about Kyle that way. Glancing at the clock on the nightstand, she figured he must be at work by now.

She stretched off her sleepiness and made her way into the master bathroom, turning on the shower spray while she brushed her teeth. When she stepped into the shower and lathered her body, she was surprised at the fullness beginning to show in her abdomen.

It was probably going to be a big baby. With a daddy over six feet tall, it was likely that their child would be good-sized. She hoped the delivery would go smoothly. But it was too soon to think about that yet.

Toweling off, she caught her reflection in the bathroom mirror. Definite beginning of a baby bump there. No disguising it under snug jeans any longer.

She suddenly remembered the jar of shea butter she'd bought at the drugstore the afternoon before. A website for expectant mothers said that rubbing it on the belly regularly throughout pregnancy might help to prevent stretch marks. When she'd checked with her friend, Leslie, she'd confirmed that many doctors and nurses recommended it to their patients who were expecting.

But where had she put the shea butter? Maybe she'd left the bag in the living room.

She pulled on her panties and bra. It was definitely time for some lingerie shopping. Even clasping the bra on the last hook was not enough to keep her growing breasts from straining to overflow the cups.

Early morning sunlight filtered through the living room windows when she stepped out of her bedroom to search for the shopping bag. Spotting it on an end table, she picked it up and then breathed in the smell of freshly-brewed coffee.

Turning toward the kitchen, she found Kyle standing shirtless in the hallway with a coffee mug in his hand and a beaming face.

"Now that's the way I like to start off my weekend." He winked at her, and his glance bee-lined straight to her torso.

"Sorry," she said, clutching the shopping bag to cover her mid-section. "I actually thought you were at work already."

"I'm off today."

"I obviously got mixed up on the days of the week, or I wouldn't have wandered out here in a bra and panties." She felt totally mortified to be parading practically nude in front of Kyle.

"Not a problem at all." He took a step toward her. "Could I ask what that dark line is that's running down from your belly button into those lacy panties you're wearing? I noticed it before you plastered that bag to your tummy, and I don't remember seeing anything like that back when we were, uh, honeymooning."

"Don't worry, it's normal. I asked Leslie. She said it sometimes appears in the third or fourth month of pregnancy. Something to do with increasing hormone levels."

"It's actually kind of cute."

"Well, it's supposed to fade after the baby arrives. You better not get too used to it."

"Now, you know I'm not taking anything for granted." He shot her his characteristic grin. "But what prompted you to venture out here first thing in the morning in your undies? I'm not complaining, mind you. Just curious."

She shook the plastic bag. "I bought some shea butter at the drugstore yesterday. It's recommended as a moisturizer during pregnancy to help prevent stretch marks."

"On your belly?"

"Well, yeah, that's the main place the skin is stretching."

"Want some help?"

What was he asking? He wanted to rub a buttery substance on her abdomen?

She didn't know whether it was the effect of those increasing hormone levels or the way Kyle looked in his jeans with his bare chest and morning stubble and mussed-up hair. Or maybe the fact that she'd been dreaming about him all night—whatever it was, she suddenly wanted nothing more than to have him caress her skin with something moist and silky.

And the sight of his broad, muscled chest wasn't doing a thing to make her think she might be making a mistake. She looked him right in the eye and handed him the shopping bag. “Sure. I could use some help.” Turning and heading into her bedroom, she heard his heavy breathing as he followed right behind her.

Before she knew it, Kyle had the lid off the jar of shea butter. Standing face-to-face with her, he tenderly fondled her tummy with the creamy mixture. His gentle strokes sent a rush of warmth right down the path of that dark line he’d mentioned.

Had he sent a similar blast of heat through her when he’d touched her in Vegas? He must have. And she didn’t think she’d be able to resist if he wanted to do more than pat her skin.

That rush of warmth diffused throughout her lower abdomen. She wanted Kyle’s touch down there, but she also longed for his mouth on hers. She wanted his skin on hers, his tongue on hers, the heat of him everywhere on her body.

“Just say the word, darlin’,” he whispered. “We can take this to the limit.”

What was stopping them? She was already pregnant, so there were no worries about contraception. And the doctor had said it was okay to have sex.

Looking into Kyle’s smoldering eyes, she searched for something that would jog her memory of the time they’d spent together in Vegas. A look, an expression he’d used, a certain way he’d touched her. But nothing seemed familiar. It was all new.

She decided that she didn’t care whether or not she remembered him from before. The past few weeks together had shown her what kind of man he was. A man she was growing to care about. The only thing she wanted now was to feel Kyle inside of her.

"I'm saying the word," she murmured. "I'm ready for you."

There was no gentle exploration, no leisurely build-up, no relaxed rhythm. It was as though they'd both been longing for this for months, and they couldn't wait a minute longer.

After that, she lost track of everything except that he was taking her somewhere she couldn't remember ever being. If she'd soared like this before, she knew it must have been with him. She just couldn't remember it. But she wasn't going to forget this time.

And then she came back to earth.

A marriage takes more than scorching sex.

There was no denying that she loved the way Kyle had just made her feel. But was she sure she loved *him*?

CHAPTER NINE

He hadn't been intending to start their Saturday morning that way. Absolutely mind-blowing sex. Even with her slightly sprouting belly, Danielle was irresistible.

Somehow the stars had aligned, and they'd both felt that magnetic pull, that desire to come together in a most intimate release.

It was as good as what he remembered from their week in Vegas. Better, actually. Because a decent amount of their honeymoon week had been spent with a what-the-hell mindset. Once they'd made love that very first night after their hot tub escapade, neither one of them wanted to spend the rest of the week together without experiencing that again.

And again.

There was no way to change the fact that they'd made love without protection that first time in Vegas. So, he'd made sure they wouldn't make that mistake a second time. By stocking up on condoms at the resort gift shop.

With each passing day, they'd felt more comfortable with each other. Developed the seeds of a friendship. Liked the way friendship and physical desire were working together. Wondered if they might have a future together.

By the end of the week, Kyle had been about ninety-seven-percent sure that he'd found his one and only. He figured Danielle had been at about eighty-five-percent certainty. She just needed to go back home to New Loudon, spend a little time around her shy and scared so-called former fiancé to confirm they were undeniably finished for good, and she'd probably decide within an hour that no one but Kyle could make her happy for the rest of her life.

Now, as he lay spooned against her derriere with his right arm draped around her torso, he was tempted to ask if what they'd done a few minutes earlier had sealed the deal for her. Had his lovemaking stirred any of those lost memories? And made her remember what had been in her heart when they'd parted in Vegas?

But he knew better than to ask those probing questions. If her memory—or any part of it—had returned as a result of their passion, she'd surely tell him. No sense frustrating her further by asking if she'd finally remembered him. Because if the answer was no, there was no point in reinforcing the disappointment.

Feeling her begin to stir, he traced protective circles over the tiny bump of her abdomen with his right hand.

Danielle let out a long sigh. “I’m not sure that was such a good idea.”

“What we just did?” He couldn’t resist pressing closer into her provocatively rounded behind. “I happen to think it was an extremely good idea. Anything that feels that amazing has got to be a good idea.”

“I’m not saying it didn’t feel good—”

“Good? That was so much more than good. Award-winning kind of feelings. Makes you want to come back for a heaping second helping kind of thing.”

“About the second helping…”

“I’m ready if you are.”

She shimmied around to face him. “If that’s what you made me feel like in Vegas, you can’t imagine how much I regret not being able to remember it.”

“I can do all kinds of new things that I guarantee you’ll never forget.” He pulled her closer.

“I doubt I’ll ever forget what happened a few minutes ago.”

“It can happen again.”

“Kyle…” She placed her palms on each side of his face and pushed him away. “I’ve got to figure out how I feel about…us. And not just in bed. The complete us. Everyday life in addition to lovemaking. It won’t work if it’s just about sex.”

“No matter how fantastic I can make you feel?”

She shook her head. “It’s not enough. There has to be something more.”

What more did she want? He’d offered to stand

by her and make sure that she and the baby received the medical care they needed. He'd offered her a place to stay while she awaited the baby's birth—and pretty much given her carte blanche to decorate the apartment however she wanted. In his mind, they'd been getting along great since they'd arrived in Cottonwood Ridge.

And he'd just proven to her that he had the goods to keep her more than satisfied in the bedroom.

What else do I have to do?

"Could you give me an idea of what that *something more* might be?" Why keep speculating about it when he could ask her outright?

Danielle squirmed, sat up in bed, yanked a quilt that was draping the footboard, and wrapped it over her shoulders. "It's not easy to define," she said.

"You couldn't possibly still be yearning for that guy Walter—"

"No, not at all."

"You told me a few things about him back in Vegas."

"I-I don't remember…"

"Something about him keeping you at arm's length for two long years," Kyle said.

"You make it sound like he pushed me away."

"Danielle, you have to admit it's not normal for a healthy young guy not to make any kind of move on an attractive woman who's supposed to be his girlfriend—"

"Walter is a gentleman. What's wrong with that?"

"For two years? Get real."

"Everyone moves at a different pace." She shrugged.

"You made a confession to me during our honeymoon," Kyle said.

"A confession? That's crazy. I can't think of anything I would've needed to confess."

"It was about Walter."

"That's impossible."

"You told me that you've always craved a sense of security—"

"Well, who doesn't?"

"You said your parents had what you called a turbulent, short-lived marriage." Kyle looked deep into her eyes. "And then you grew up watching your mother struggle to raise you virtually alone. And she wouldn't have made it without help from Nana Rose."

"I'm not the only kid who grew up that way."

"I know, but you admitted that it left you with an almost overwhelming fear of an unstable, unreliable husband."

"No woman wants a husband like that."

"But most women wouldn't settle for an incredibly boring man just because he had a stable income and almost no desire to wander from home."

"What are you talking about?" Danielle's eyes blazed.

"Come on, you know I just described Walter Ferguson right down to his socks."

"Incredibly boring?"

"Uh, yeah, I'd say so." Kyle grinned. "Pretty much the most unexciting guy in the state of

Colorado, but you told me his family owns an upholstery business that's virtually cornered the market for re-covering Western-style furniture in a good part of the southwestern region of the country. Plus a few big-ticket contracts with hotels and resorts."

"How do you know all that?"

"You told me when we were in Vegas." Kyle cocked his head. "And you said when his father passed away a few years ago, Walter stepped up to be the head honcho. The self-proclaimed King of Colorado Chair Cushions."

"You could've easily found all of that out by searching on the internet."

"But I didn't have to, because you told me."

Danielle opened her mouth to respond, but before she could answer, her phone buzzed on the night table. They both looked at the phone as Walter Ferguson's name lit up the screen.

"What the hell is he calling you for?" Kyle struggled not to explode as he ground his teeth.

Could he actually be competing with this guy to win back the heart of his own wife? It was insane. And even more insane was that Walter had never even seemed to want Danielle's heart. The way Danielle had explained it during their honeymoon, Walter was laser-focused on showing his mother that he could make their upholstery business even more successful than his father had. Didn't she remember that?

But that car accident had robbed her of the feelings that had grown during the time she'd spent with Kyle. Now he had to convince her that he was in love with her for all the right reasons.

And after that, he had to convince himself that she had fallen back in love with him for all the right reasons.

* * *

Danielle gaped at her phone and Walter's name flashing at her. He hadn't called her once in the six months she was in California. And she'd only briefly seen him twice that she recalled since returning to Colorado. Why would he call her now?

"Let it go to voicemail," Kyle said. "Whatever it is can wait."

"What if it's about Nana Rose?"

"Why would *he* be calling you about it?"

Danielle reached for the phone, and Kyle firmly covered her hand with his. "If it's important, he'll leave a message," he said, and stared hard at her. "We just made love a few minutes ago. You don't need to talk to him now."

She had to admit he was right. If something had happened with Nana Rose, someone from the Ponderosa Manor Apartments would call her. Or Leslie would call. She worked at the hospital and knew just about everything that happened within its walls.

But what if Nana Rose actually were in the hospital?

Stop letting your imagination go wild. If she were, Walter wouldn't be the one to notify you.

"You're right." Danielle turned away from the night table and the phone that had finally stopped buzzing. "It's just that Nana is getting up in years, and I worry that something could happen to her."

"She looked pretty healthy to me."

"So, now you're a doctor?"

"I'm only saying that she seems very active, especially for…how old is Nana Rose, anyway?"

"She turned seventy a few months ago."

"In today's world, that's not necessarily old." Kyle patted her shoulder. "Still, I understand how you'd worry about your grandmother, especially since she pretty much raised you. Why don't you check in with her later?"

Kyle didn't know that she'd promised to text Nana twice a day to confirm she was safe with him. This probably wasn't a good time to tell him about that arrangement. "Yeah, I'll do that."

He slid his hand from her shoulder to beneath the quilt she clutched over her breasts and pulled her snugly against him. "You still haven't told me what that *something more* is that you're looking for."

His caress set her tingling again. Was she making the biggest mistake of her life by telling Kyle that he needed to do more than take her breath away, send electric sparks through her core, and leave her desperate for more?

Take a deep breath, and let the butterflies inside you settle down.

Baby between them or not, she wasn't going to let physical hunger guide her decision-making process. Maybe she'd done that when she first met Kyle. She had no idea what had prompted her to make those decisions back in the heat of summer.

"You and I got off to a crazy start. There's no

other way to describe it." She couldn't imagine any sane person describing the way they'd ended up married as anything but irrational, senseless, even foolish. "But we don't have to keep acting that way. For the sake of our child's future, we need to act responsibly. Make sure we're truly suited for each other."

"I think you're still not sure I can give you the security you were looking for with Walter."

"Wait—what?" She recoiled as though she'd come up against a cement wall. "Why are we still talking about Walter?"

"Nobody has to say anything. He's the elephant in the room. A big gray mass right in the middle of everything, but you keep looking the other way and pretending not to see it."

Had Walter been that important to her? She'd known him most of her life, gone to school with him, and gotten friendly after they'd both returned home to New Loudon after college. People started calling them a couple. She started calling him her fiancé. And he called her his fiancée too.

Didn't he?

Now, she couldn't remember for sure.

A lot of details about Walter seemed kind of blurry. Why did she call him her fiancé if they'd never actually discussed marriage? The closest they'd come was when she'd occasionally throw in a reference to *after we're married...* And now that she thought about it, Walter had usually found a way to change the subject.

Another tiny drop of water broke free from that mental ice cube.

Danielle had finished packing the last of her possessions into her car before leaving L.A. And she'd been dreading the inevitable I-told-you-so lecture from Walter when she arrived back in Colorado. She could almost hear his voice. *Did you finally get it out of your system, Danielle? Now are you ready to settle down and focus on being a teacher?*

Her decision to take a break from her super-reliable teaching job to try to make it big in Hollywood had probably been her way of seeing if there were something else out there for her. But she was sure she'd had no intention of trying to heat things up with Walter when she got back to Colorado. It was firm in her mind the whole time she'd been in California that she was done waiting for him to show some interest.

Was that why she'd so quickly glommed on to Kyle when their paths had crossed?

"I'm not sure you should refer to Walter as an elephant…" she eventually said, shaking her head.

"You know what I mean. You're an English teacher, for God's sake. Don't you teach your students about metaphors?"

"Of course, I do. But I usually come up with more abstract examples. I rarely refer to someone we actually know as an elephant. Or use any derogatory term."

"I guess I shouldn't have compared this to a classroom exercise. Because this is a real-life, grown-up problem."

"Look, I don't care about Walter anymore. I haven't for a long time. And are you saying that us getting to know each other better before we focus so much on sex is a problem?" If she'd jumped in too quickly in Vegas, she didn't want to repeat her mistake. "Isn't that the way it's normally done?"

"Nothing about us is normal. Our relationship has been unusual from the moment we met." He threw up his hands. "And I'm fine with us getting to know each other better. What happened between us this morning was chemistry…like an explosion in the lab when two heated chemicals get too close and nature takes its course."

She pulled away from his embrace. "Maybe we need to dial it back for a while to make things a little more cookie-cutter."

"Is that what you think will solve everything? Because I already know I want to stay married to you." He sent Danielle a look that tore at her insides. "But I'm not sure you feel the same way about me."

* * *

Kyle imagined a version of dialing their relationship back that was probably not the same as Danielle's idea. And he'd never been much for baking, so he had no interest in anything to do with cookie cutters.

"It's Saturday, and I've got the whole day off from work. Here's what I think." He swept his fingertips along her jawline. "You and I should go on a date."

"A date? But we're already living together." Danielle scrunched her eyebrows.

"So, let's get out of the house and enjoy what

this town's got to offer."

"Such as?"

Kyle tilted his head from side to side. "There's an outdoor craft show downtown. They've got something like fifty artists displaying their work. A lot of them are staying at my resort."

"A kickoff to the holiday season? I can get with that."

Thirty minutes later, Kyle parked his Explorer downtown, and he and Danielle walked a couple blocks to the town square, now lined with artists' booths. "Beautiful weather for this event," he said. "I understand they hold it whether or not it snows."

"The leaves that have turned yellow look gorgeous." She motioned to the backdrop of the mountain.

"We better enjoy the fall colors while we can. I've been told the first snowfall is late this year and could be any day."

"You'll have to get used to it, California Boy." Danielle grinned.

"California by way of Texas, you forget."

Danielle's face darkened. "I've forgotten a lot of things lately."

"Oh man, I don't know why I keep making jokes about you forgetting things." What was wrong with him? He needed to strike the words *forget, remember,* and *memory* from his vocabulary for a while.

"I get it. You sometimes use expressions that people say without thinking." She shrugged. "No offense taken."

"C'mon, let's check out what these artists have

for sale." He clutched her hand and steered her toward a crowded booth where a man in weathered jeans and a vintage Led Zeppelin t-shirt offered photographs of local scenery.

"Beautiful," Danielle murmured.

"Yeah, we could consider something like that to decorate our apartment."

"There are too many to choose from." She crossed her arms across her chest. "I couldn't decide right now."

Kyle scanned the surrounding booths and slipped his arm around her shoulders. "I want to see what that vendor's selling."

They ambled across the square to a booth filled with hand-made jewelry. He was instantly drawn to a heart-shaped sterling silver locket on a chain. A blue stone glittered from the center of the ornately-carved heart.

A slender, pony-tailed woman in jeans behind the counter stepped toward them. "You have good taste. It's all hand-made. By me," she said to him, and then turned to Danielle. "Would you like to try it on?"

"Oh, I'm not sure." Danielle glanced at him, her eyes looking nervous.

He ran a finger over the locket and turned to the woman in the booth. "What's the blue stone in the middle?"

"Topaz. It's considered the gemstone for the fourth wedding anniversary." The woman glanced at Danielle's left ring finger, which was bare of jewelry.

"We haven't even reached the first anniversary

yet." He laughed and turned to Danielle. "Do you like it?"

"It's exquisite, but—"

He dropped his voice. "While you're waiting to put that wedding ring back on, this would be a nice piece of jewelry for you to wear."

Danielle tilted her head toward the woman. "But she said it's for the fourth wedding anniversary."

"So, when did we ever do anything in the right order?" He motioned for the woman behind the booth to take the necklace from the display. "Let's see how it looks on you, darlin'."

The woman undid the lobster claw clasp, fastened the necklace around Danielle's neck, and held a mirror in front of her.

"Oh, my goodness," Danielle gushed. "It really is beautiful."

"The topaz is the same color as your eyes," the woman said, and then discreetly showed Kyle a card with the price.

"It does light up your eyes," Kyle said to Danielle, who placed her right hand atop her breasts as she stared at the necklace in the mirror.

"I can take ten percent off the price," the woman said, leaning closer to him.

"We'll take it, and she'll wear it right now." He squeezed Danielle's shoulders and planted a light kiss on her mouth. "You look gorgeous."

"Thank you—for that compliment and for the stunning necklace."

Her eyes sparkled, and he wondered if love—for him—was behind the gleam.

They spent the next hour wandering from booth to booth, taking in displays of carved wood, copper pieces, paintings and drawings, blown glass, sculptures, ceramics, and elaborately-styled handbags. "There's so much talent around here," Kyle said.

"It must be an artistic community," she agreed.

He couldn't help noticing a few times when Danielle caught sight of her reflection in a mirror or shop window and focused her gaze on the new necklace around her neck. Even if she wouldn't wear the wedding ring he'd given her in Vegas, he felt good seeing her wear a piece of jewelry he'd picked out just for her.

And he was going to make sure she would willingly put that wedding ring back on her finger soon.

Why was it taking her so long to figure out what she'd pretty much nailed in the first week they'd met? They were meant to be together.

He was sure her indecision played into his delay in letting his parents and sister know about the baby. He fully expected them to be furious when they found out he'd been married for about three months…and had been a father-to-be for that same amount of time.

Maybe fury wasn't the exact emotion he'd expect them to display. Shock would be more like it.

But he expected they'd soften up over the prospect of a new baby in the family. Especially his mother. He wouldn't be surprised if she hired a skywriter to announce the happy news to the good citizens of Austin, Texas.

He expected his sister Samantha to be thrilled as well. There might be some initial resistance from his father. Particularly after that broken engagement when Kyle's fiancée had decided he wasn't quite worth marrying if he wasn't willing to move right into a high-paying executive position with his parents' company. That had made his dad a little gun-shy around prospective daughters-in-law. "Watch out for gold diggers," he'd warned Kyle on more than one occasion.

Danielle wasn't doing any gold digging. At least not with him. Look at the way he'd had to convince her to accept a necklace as a gift from him.

Even so, he wasn't ready to go into full-disclosure mode about the size of his parents' business empire. If she decided to make a go of things with him, Kyle wanted to be sure it was because she was so in love with him that she couldn't imagine herself with anyone else, and not just so she wouldn't have to worry about the bills getting paid.

The next evening, Kyle returned from work exhausted. When Danielle greeted him at the door in a tiered top that concealed her growing tummy but not the increasing mound of her breasts, he was desperate to hear her say that she'd realized—beyond a doubt—that he was the love of her life.

Ping! An announcement that, just like that, the fog had cleared from her brain, and everything had become clear. All the sweet things he had been doing for nearly a month had dislodged whatever had blocked her memory of their time in Vegas. She'd connected the dots, put two and two together, had a light bulb go on in her brain—however you'd describe that moment of epiphany when Kyle emerged in her consciousness as her true love.

Instead, her face lit up as she fingered the heart pendant with the topaz stone. "Thank you again for this beautiful necklace," she said. "That was super thoughtful of you."

"I like giving you pretty things." He kissed her, and she returned it, letting the kiss linger a little longer than the light one they'd exchanged yesterday at the art show. His senses filled with her fresh scent, and he couldn't help wishing she would excitedly announce she'd had a grand awakening of her forgotten memories.

But when she broke the kiss, Danielle didn't declare that she'd had a memory breakthrough. "I sincerely appreciate the gift," she said, stroking the pendant again and then biting her lip. "And I was wondering today if you've come up with a good way to inform your family about me. And about our baby."

"No, but I guess it's time that I got around to that." To be honest, the time had come and gone, and each passing day where he didn't come clean to his parents ramped up the likelihood that the announcement wouldn't go smoothly.

"Do you think they'd like to come here to meet me and see where we live?"

"I'm sure they would. It'd just be a matter of their schedules. They're a couple of extremely busy folks."

"Right, what with their restaurant and everything." Danielle nodded in understanding. "It's probably hard to even take a day off from making sure everything's running smoothly in the kitchen and all those kinds of things."

"Well, um, yeah." He still didn't think it was the time to tell her that his parents were more concerned with corporate-level operations than the day-to-day management of a single restaurant.

Make her fall back in love with me first, and then I can spring the multi-millionaire status of my folks on her.

Glancing down the hallway in the direction of the spare bedroom that he still occupied, he wondered how his parents would react if they dropped in and realized their son wasn't even sleeping with his bride. His pregnant bride.

That would be some kind of visit.

CHAPTER TEN

The next morning, Danielle was pleased when Kyle dusted her cheek with a friendly kiss before leaving for work and promised to call his parents later that day.

She expected it would be a difficult phone call. To say the least.

Telling Nana Rose about the whirlwind marriage and unexpected pregnancy had been about as easy for Danielle as turning a backflip with her newly-blossoming tummy would be at that very moment.

And she'd been less than two months along when she'd given Nana the news. Plus, she'd only found out about it herself that same day. So, she hadn't specifically been keeping a secret from her grandmother for a long time.

But Kyle was in a different situation with his family. He'd been married for almost three months now. And he'd known he was going to be a dad for a good part of that time.

His parents might not take too kindly to the late-breaking nature of the news. And whose fault was that? She had to admit that she was the one who said she needed time to decide if she wanted to make their marriage permanent.

But she couldn't be blamed for getting hit by an out-of-control vehicle and ending up a victim of partial amnesia.

It suddenly occurred to her that the longer she and Kyle lived together, the harder it might be to get the marriage annulled. If that's what they eventually decided to do.

A real live baby and several months of living together sure looked like a legitimate marriage.

Maybe not the part that took place in the bedroom. Or didn't take place in the bedroom. Or had taken place one time in the bedroom since they'd moved to this apartment.

Gentle prickles of pleasure teased her with the memory of Kyle's blazing touch.

Why am I thinking about him that way? I made up my mind that we need to forge a solid emotional connection first. Molten sex is not going to form the foundation for my marriage.

She involuntarily shivered, almost trying to shake off the tingles skittering through her. When her cell phone rang, it yanked her back into the moment. Expecting to see the name of Leslie or Nana…or maybe even Kyle…on her smartphone display, she was surprised when a different name appeared on the screen.

Mark Zanderman. Her agent from back in L.A.

The guy who'd landed her the small part in the movie. The one where the only acting skills required were to give the impression of being bored while reclining totally nude in a floating lounger.

What could he want with her? A miniscule glimmer of hope that she might get paid for showing up on set that day—even though she'd left before going through with getting naked and hopping in the swimming pool—made her answer Mark's call.

"Danielle!" Mark's booming voice assaulted her eardrums. "Hey, I've got good news for you."

What? No asking how she was or anything so trivial as social niceties? That's right, Mark was a busy Hollywood agent, locking down deals for all kinds of big players in the movie industry.

Like a quick peep at a young woman's breasts…and other body parts usually reserved for a lover…while she was partially submerged in water. Real Oscar-worthy material.

"Nice to talk to you too, Mark," she said, not sure whether she wanted to disguise or flaunt the sarcasm that most likely was filtering into her voice.

"Oh, right." Mark hesitated for something like a nanosecond before launching into his spiel. "Yeah, remember that part you didn't get?"

"Which one? There were so many, I'm having trouble keeping track."

"Working title was *Her Bottom Line*. Kind of a double entendre there. Romantic comedy about a—shall we say—model who takes over a huge business in a mistaken identity thing."

"How could that even happen?"

"I'm not talking about a documentary. It's a classic fish out of water story. And it ends with the—like I said—model ending up being smarter than all the MBAs in charge of the company. She increases the bottom line—the profits—more than any of those other Einsteins ever did."

"Heartwarming," Danielle responded, not even trying to hide her sarcastic tone. "But why are you calling me about it? I didn't get the part."

"You weren't even up for the lead role, Darlene."

"Danielle," she corrected.

"Right, right," Mark mumbled.

And was she supposed to feel better because she couldn't lose out on the lead role, since she hadn't even been considered for it in the first place? Mark was rubbing in that she couldn't even get hired for bit parts. Unless they required stripping for the camera.

"What's your point, Mark?"

"I'm telling you they're interested in you. You auditioned for the part of the model's best friend from the old days. She's a hot-looking thing who never went to business school either but has a lot of common sense about how things should be done. And she kind of keeps the lead actress grounded when there's a danger all the money she's making might go to her head."

"They want me to play the hot-looking best friend who's also brilliant but doesn't have an MBA either?"

"That's almost it. Their original choice for the role didn't work out. Then they reviewed the audition tapes, and you've got a callback. Tomorrow morning at ten. Can you get here?"

She'd need to be in L.A. in less than twenty-four hours. This could be the break she'd been dreaming of. But could she even get there in time?

Her sarcastic tone turned regretful. "I'm not sure…"

"What do you mean, you're not sure? Honestly, I think you've got this one in the bag. It's not a huge part, but it could lead to something bigger."

"Mark, I don't—"

"Look, you have the acting chops." He cleared his throat. "Full disclosure, the character wears tight-fitting, skimpy outfits. But there's no nudity. It's absolutely perfect for you."

Tight-fitting, skimpy outfits.

Without needing to think, her hand went to her abdomen. The baby. Growing bigger each day. Even if she somehow managed to get to the audition the next day, she doubted she'd be able to hide the swelling of her tummy in the skimpy outfit they'd surely want her to wear before they made their final decision.

And if she somehow actually got the part, by the time filming was underway, every scene would reveal her baby growing larger with each passing day.

"It sounds great, Mark," she heard herself saying. "But I guess you didn't know I was in a pretty bad car accident about a week after I left L.A."

* * *

Kyle had barely gotten in the door after work that evening when Danielle started talking about wanting to get a job while she awaited the baby's birth.

"How come?" He couldn't imagine what had popped that idea into her head. But he was relieved that she didn't immediately grill him about revealing their situation to his parents and sister.

"I'm not someone who likes to have nothing to do," she explained to him. "I'm used to being active. Teaching, advising the high school drama club, auditioning for acting parts… I've spent way too much time the past couple of months taking things easy."

"Do I need to remind you that you were in a serious car accident that wiped out a portion of your memory?"

"No reminder necessary." Danielle shrugged. "But I'm dealing with it."

"On top of that, then you had to deal with feeling all worn out and nauseous from the pregnancy." He approached her where she sat at the dining table with several books and magazines about pregnancy spread before her, and squeezed her shoulders. "You more than deserve a little break from concentrating on lesson plans and standing on your feet a good part of the day."

"That's what I've had—a little break. And now I'm feeling better, and I need to be more active." She flipped one of the books shut. "All of these books and articles say it's good to keep on the go while you're expecting."

"But the school year is well underway, so I doubt you'd find an opening for an English teacher at the local high school."

"You're probably right, but teaching isn't the only thing I can do. I worked as a waitress while I was in L.A.—in between auditions and rejections." A hint of a smile appeared on her face, and she motioned for him to look at a picture of an adorably chubby-cheeked infant on the cover of one of the magazines.

"Aww, I hope our baby is that cute," he said.

"Have you looked in the mirror?" Danielle winked at him. "This baby can't help but be cute."

He snorted and then said, "Okay, I'm officially taking all the credit for any good looks."

"Anyway, there has to be some kind of work in this town for me. Even part-time would be fine."

Kyle had to admit that she had a point. It was close to six months before the baby was scheduled to arrive. Straightening up a two-bedroom apartment and cooking dinner every night left a whole lot of room for other more fulfilling undertakings.

As long as whatever it was didn't adversely affect her pregnancy or take away from his efforts to improve their relationship. It was already enough of a struggle to restore it to full-blown romance instead of this on again-off again deal they seemed to have going.

"That might not be such a bad idea," he conceded. "Do you want me to ask around at the resort? Someone there might know about a part-time opening in town. With ski season approaching, businesses will be hiring."

Her eyes lit up. "That would be great. And I'll check around too. I like our team approach to job hunting."

Did she consider them to be a team? But what kind of team? Sure, it would be great to work together toward a common goal. But students or co-workers could do that kind of thing.

He wanted to be on a different kind of team with her. A two-person team that could accomplish all sorts of great things. But they'd celebrate their victories in a more intimate way.

Danielle had enjoyed their lovemaking on Saturday morning. He was certain of it. But something held her back from fully accepting him as her husband. It might be that she still needed to get to know him better.

Maybe if he finally introduced her to his family, it would show her that he was serious about their relationship. This wasn't a temporary fling for him. He had no devious plan to have as much casual sex with her as possible until the baby was born and then decide he'd rather be an absentee dad.

"Okay, we'll put our heads together and see which employer in this town is going to be lucky enough to hire you." Kyle smiled, and then his face turned reflective. "Did something happen today that made you decide you needed to ratchet up your activity level?"

The change of expression on her face told him that something had indeed happened that day.

When she told him about the call from her

agent, a sickening sensation crept into his gut. She wasn't thinking about running back to Hollywood, was she? He couldn't bear it if she was using him as a stopgap until she landed that elusive movie part she'd been searching for.

And when she explained that she wouldn't be able to take the part anyway because of her expanding tummy, Kyle's sickening sensation morphed into outright piercing pain. Could she be using him as a makeshift husband until the baby was delivered and she got her pre-pregnancy figure back again? Then she'd rev up again for a second try at her big dream?

But as she got further into the story of the call from her agent, Kyle's aching slowly eased.

Her mouth twisted, and she shook her head in disgust as she related Mark Zanderman's reaction when she told him about her car accident. "Can you believe the first thing he asked was whether I'd gotten any scars from the crash? Not a word about how I was feeling or if there were any lingering after-effects."

"Like amnesia?"

"I didn't even tell him about that. Why give him more ammunition to label me as damaged goods?"

"What about being pregnant?"

She quickly glanced sideways and then met Kyle's gaze. "I didn't tell him about the baby."

"The baby is a pretty big deal."

"It's not that I'm ashamed or anything like that." Danielle waved a hand. "But I didn't think it was his business."

"The way you were talking about him a minute ago, I thought you were going to tell me you declined the callback." His throat tightened as he imagined her telling him something that would upend their fledgling marriage. "How did you finish the conversation with him?"

He waited for her to tell him that she'd let her agent know that she wouldn't reconsider her decision to give up on trying to make it big in Hollywood. That she'd found something a whole lot better on her way home. Except she didn't exactly remember what she'd found, but she was oh-so-close to discovering it again. If only she'd let Kyle in—into her heart, her mind, her body.

But she tossed her hair and took a long sip of ice water. "Oh, I turned down the callback audition. It kind of broke my heart. Death of a dream and all that."

"But you have something good now, right?" All he wanted was to hear her tell him that she was happy to be his wife, happy to be having his baby, happy to be living with him in a nice town at the base of picturesque mountains. He didn't want to feel like the leftovers that were grudgingly eaten when nothing better was available.

Beaming, she placed a hand on her belly. "I have something that's more than good. But there's nothing wrong with keeping the door open for future opportunities."

"What do you mean?"

"I told Mark Zanderman that I'm fine, but my doctor doesn't want me to take on anything new for a while. So, I couldn't even think about changing my mind about being an actress until sometime in the second part of next year."

"After the baby's born?"

"Exactly."

Now, he wasn't sure how he should feel. Because it sure sounded like Danielle might be intending to dump him for one more chance at stardom. Was she only interested in him as a source of child support for their baby?

* * *

Danielle had hoped Kyle would be excited to hear of her plans to search for a part-time job in town for the next few months. But he sat across from her looking downright glum.

Was he upset because she hadn't flat out told her agent that she'd never even so much as consider an acting part again? No matter how lucrative it might be.

What was wrong about keeping her options open? Plenty of actresses juggled career, kids, husbands, and even side businesses. Maybe she could do it too. Why would she slam the door on the potential of a big opportunity down the road?

Trying to keep her tone light, she decided to switch gears and broach the subject of Kyle's family. "Did you get the chance to call your parents today?"

"I did."

"And how did it go?"

"Pretty much as expected." His jaw tightened, but then he smiled. "I was able to conference them both in, so they could hear the news at the same time. I think they were shocked that I've been married for a couple of months, disappointed that they weren't at the ceremony, but happy to hear that they're going to be grandparents for the first time."

"They were genuinely happy? Even though they don't know anything about me."

"Well, they know something about you now."

"What did you tell them?" She wondered what kind of spin Kyle had put on the story about the car breakdown in Barstow, the fake marriage that resulted in pregnancy, and her partial amnesia. "The story's so wild that you couldn't even make it up if you tried."

"Let's just say that I didn't elaborate on *every* detail of the first week that we met. I was a little vague about how and when we first connected, simply saying that you're from Colorado but had been working in L.A. We decided to elope in Vegas, but then we weren't sure if we'd done the right thing. Which is why I hadn't told them about us right away."

"And they were okay with that?"

"Uh, there's nothing they can do about it now. And they got pretty excited when I let them know about the baby."

"Even though *we're* not sure if we did the right thing?"

"I said that when we found out that you were pregnant, we realized we wanted to be a couple and a family. And everything's great."

"I'm sorry if I caused you to have to lie to your parents."

"Which part of it are you considering to be a

lie? Because I'm thinking it's more of embroidering the truth a little. Or maybe leaving out a small detail here and there."

Had she heard something wrong, or had he said that he'd told his parents that she and Kyle wanted to be a couple and a family? And that everything was great. And that none of it was a lie.

Because she had been thinking that they were on more of the trial marriage option. But maybe he thought their overall relationship was, in fact, great. Even she had to admit she felt much better about it than when they'd first moved in together.

Then again, whose life was changing more as a result of what had happened in Vegas? He'd probably be at this new job in Cottonwood Ridge no matter what. The only difference was that he was here with a wife who made sure he had a nice dinner every evening. And had let him make love to her that one amazing time since they'd arrived in town.

But she was the one whose body was changing. Changing in ways that wouldn't allow her to audition for that movie role even if she'd wanted to. And she didn't like not being able to make her own decisions.

No matter what happened between Kyle and her, she was the one who would be primarily responsible for caring for their baby. Her life was never going to be the same. And she might have somehow managed to arrange for it to be as much of a struggle as her mother had dealt with.

Broken marriage and single motherhood.

Why didn't Kyle realize that she had more at

stake in this situation than he did?

But she wasn't ready to do any soul searching with him right now. "You're right," she finally replied. "Simply embroidering the truth."

And she left it at that.

CHAPTER ELEVEN

Danielle had thought finding a part-time job would be a shoo-in, but it turned out to be anything but.

Over the next few days, she checked out the various shops, restaurants, and other businesses in the main part of town. While many of them were hiring extra help for the winter season, none of the openings seemed right.

Either a decent amount of moderately heavy lifting was included with the regular duties, or there wouldn't be enough flexibility in scheduling to permit Danielle to go to her prenatal doctor visits or occasionally visit Nana Rose back in New Loudon.

By mid-day the following Monday, it seemed she'd exhausted every potential temporary opportunity in town, and a cloud of defeat appeared to be hovering above her head. The only really positive thing that had happened in the past few days was using her car insurance check for a down payment on a new vehicle, an SUV crossover that could handle Colorado snow with a baby safely strapped into a car seat in the back.

Longing for someone or something that smacked of optimism, she called Kyle's cell. A dose of his ever-present upbeat attitude was exactly what she needed to lift her out of the doldrums.

He answered on the second ring. "Is everything okay?"

"Hello to you too."

"Sorry for being abrupt. I can't help worrying about you and the baby."

"I think you worry too much."

"You're both important to me," he said. "That's why my nerves jumped when I saw an unexpected call from you."

"Everything's fine." She cleared her throat. "At least health-wise. It's trying to find a part-time job that's getting me down."

"It's almost time for my lunch break. Can you stop by the resort? I have a big pair of shoulders you can cry on."

He probably did have the broadest shoulders she'd ever seen. Then she reminded herself not to focus on his sex appeal, but to think of him as a supportive mate in an unfamiliar town.

Pulling up to the resort a few minutes later, she took in the impressive main building, a stone and stucco structure reminiscent of a European ski lodge. When she entered the lobby, she was struck by its old-world charm. Everything about the space, from the deep burgundy and cream color palette, to the rough-hewn ceiling beams and Aubusson rugs covering the tumbled marbled floor, evoked a sense of luxury steeped in comfort.

What a nice place for Kyle to come to work every day. How did he spend the best part of his waking hours in this stylish environment and then manage to enjoy coming home to their modest apartment?

Maybe he didn't enjoy coming home.

And it probably didn't help that his wife wasn't sure if she wanted to remain married to him. Definitely didn't help that his wife wouldn't let him make love to her on a regular basis.

Well, she'd let him that one time after he'd rubbed the shea butter over her belly and made it next to impossible for her to resist him. But it wasn't totally accurate to say that she'd *let him* make love to her that Saturday morning. Because she'd wanted it every bit as much as he had.

And she wanted them to do the same thing again.

Danielle forced herself to stop thinking about that feeling when Kyle made love to her. Yes, it was nice, it was delightful, it was amazing. But a lot of it was a physiological reaction. True, Kyle was probably a lot better than most men at setting off and sustaining that kind of reaction. But no matter how astounding his lovemaking talents were, that wasn't enough to ensure the long-term success of their marriage.

They needed to keep working on their relationship. She had to be sure that during the week they'd spent together in Vegas, she liked Kyle as a person and figured out they had a lot in common. It would be devastating if she realized that whole experience had only been about making money.

When he suddenly appeared in a doorway off the hotel lobby, she felt almost embarrassed by some of the thoughts she'd been having about him. But she couldn't stop the fluttering in her stomach when Kyle got as near to her as he was now, saying something about getting lunch in the resort's casual restaurant that faced the mountain.

The man certainly had some kind of effect on her. She was losing track of everything but his closeness.

"Whatever they're cooking smells tempting," she said, trying to reconnect herself to her surroundings as Kyle ushered her into the restaurant, where several guests were seated. Floor to ceiling windows provided a spectacular vista, with the mountain dominating the view.

"I'm working with the executive chef to tweak the menus, but there's certainly no need for a major overhaul." Kyle's face showed a touch of pride. "It's rare that we receive a complaint about the food here."

She could see that making the resort a success was important to him. And as the hostess seated them at a table next to the windows, Danielle felt a tiny sliver of ice breaking away from that frozen area of her brain. Something about making it on his own and being a success in his own right. Kyle had said something like that to her—but where and when?

An image of Kyle sitting across from her at a table in front of a window glided past her vision.

The window was huge, similar to the one beside their table now, but the view was completely different. Instead of the hill dotted with spruces that was in front of them now, she could see Kyle seated at a table, a glass of red wine in his hand, with a manicured garden visible through the glass behind him.

It must have been during their honeymoon. Having dinner at that resort where they'd stayed. And he was saying something about disappointing his parents.

"Would you like iced tea? Or is a glass of ice water okay?" Kyle's voice cut into the vision trying to break through her scrambled memory, and she looked up to see a young man at their table, apparently trying to take their beverage order.

"Ice water will be fine," she said, wondering what else she'd missed while she'd been trying to recall that earlier conversation with Kyle. It was so close to the surface, nearly ready to emerge into a place where she could easily retrieve it whenever she wanted. But it had submerged itself again.

"So, listen," Kyle said, after the server reviewed the lunch specials and then disappeared into the kitchen to get their drinks. "I know you're kind of down because you haven't been able to line up a part-time job as easily as you'd hoped. But please don't feel that you have to get a job for financial reasons. My job here at the resort will cover our bills."

"I appreciate your generosity." She smiled, and then her expression became serious. "But I need something to occupy my time. To keep me intellectually challenged too. I can't see myself spending the next few months straightening up our apartment."

"Understood." He nodded. "Don't give up your job search. Even if you can't find a paying job, maybe there's an opportunity for some volunteer work. An extra paycheck is really not an issue right now."

"I hadn't thought of volunteer work. I guess I feel weird not bringing home a paycheck."

How could she ask for a husband to be more supportive? She wasn't sure if she imagined it, but she swore she felt the slightest tingle when he touched her hand. Static electricity? Or was she falling in love with him again?

How had it happened in Las Vegas? Would she ever remember what she'd felt, sensed, tasted when she'd fallen in love with Kyle during that lost week? She must have fallen in love with him. And he must have fallen in love with her too. Otherwise, when they'd found out she was pregnant, wouldn't he have told her that he'd ante up the child support but wasn't in for the living together and bringing up baby deal?

She wasn't even sure what falling in love was supposed to feel like. It had definitely never happened to her before that week in Vegas. Maybe it had happened that week with Kyle. Whether it had or not, it was happening to her now.

Stealing a glance at him as he studied the menu, she wondered how he really felt about her.

He glanced up and met her gaze. "Everything okay? You look deep in thought."

Uncomfortable that she'd been thinking about his true feelings for her, she mumbled, "I was just thinking about what kind of volunteer opportunities might be available."

Trying to set aside her tangle of thoughts, she focused on the menu and then on her grilled chicken sandwich. It was nice sitting with her husband, enjoying a meal, talking about everyday things. It would be even nicer if they were also anticipating making sweet love later that night. She forced herself to stop letting her thoughts drift that way.

Focus on our emotional connection. Can I be sure he's in love with me too? Then the sexual relationship will be the natural result.

So, she complimented the restaurant food and atmosphere. She asked if it looked like business would be good at the resort during the upcoming winter season. She told Kyle she'd heard some women at the grocery store talking about the spa at the resort, so it must be popular with locals as well as out-of-town guests.

"Would you like to go to a movie one night this week?" Kyle asked when they were almost finished with their meal. "There's a new thriller out, and I know how much you like them."

"How would you know—" She brought herself up short. "Was that something you found out about me during our honeymoon?"

He nodded. "That, and many other things."

"And you want to see the movie too?"

"Absolutely."

Everything was easy and comfortable by the time their server offered them the dessert menu and left them to review the selections. “Vanilla or chocolate ice cream,” Danielle commented. “I don’t know why, but I’ve been craving coffee-chocolate chip ice cream the past few days.”

Kyle smirked. “You don’t know why? I’d guess it’s because you’re pregnant. Aren’t cravings fairly common when you’re expecting?”

“I guess so. I hadn’t even thought about it.” She’d been doing so much thinking about how things were going to work out with Kyle that she’d hadn’t connected her sudden desire for a specific flavor of ice cream with a classic longing for a particular food that many expectant mothers experienced.

Still trying to decide whether to indulge in a more ordinary flavor of ice cream, Danielle looked up to see a mature woman in a business suit crossing the room.

Kyle signaled to her, and the woman with flattering streaks of silver in her dark hair smiled as she approached their table. He introduced Sheila Clayton as the resort’s executive housekeeper, and she shook hands with Danielle.

“I hope you’re enjoying your lunch,” Sheila said.

Danielle nodded. “Delicious food and wonderful ambience here. It’s all helping to keep my mind off my bad luck at job hunting. I’m striking out big-time at finding a part-time job in town.”

“Really?” Sheila appeared thoughtful. “I believe your husband mentioned one time that you’re a certified high school teacher?”

"Yes, I taught English for several years at New Loudon High." She shrugged. "But it's already well into the fall semester. And I wouldn't be able to work full-time for the entire year anyway."

"My daughter-in-law is the principal at Cottonwood Ridge High. Would you like me to ask her if there are any temporary opportunities there? It's a small school, but they do need substitute teachers sometimes."

Danielle's eyes met Kyle's, and he nodded in agreement. It looked like they both thought that this might be the perfect opportunity for her. Occasional work that would be worthwhile. And with no heavy lifting required.

After Sheila Clayton promised to check in with her daughter-in-law, Danielle relaxed and enjoyed a tiny serving of chocolate ice cream. "It's not coffee-chocolate chip, but a pretty decent substitute."

Walking through the lobby with Kyle a few minutes later, she was ready to say good-bye when the executive housekeeper hurriedly approached them.

"Mrs. Williams," she said to Danielle, "I just spoke to my daughter-in-law. If you can meet her at the high school at three o'clock this afternoon, she'd like to talk to you about filling in for a teacher who is having surgery on Monday. He'll be out all next week, and they haven't been able to find a substitute who can cover all five days."

It hadn't been what she'd been planning, but maybe this substitute teaching opportunity would work out for the best. For one thing, it'd give her something to do in addition to keeping a small apartment clean and preparing meals. Secondly, it would bring in some extra income and make her feel that she was contributing financially to the marriage. And probably most importantly, it would keep her in the game as far as the teaching profession went.

If things didn't work out with Kyle, she would need a good job to raise a baby on her own.

* * *

The following Monday, Danielle had a mild case of jitters as she parked in the high school parking lot, set to begin her first substitute teaching assignment at Cottonwood Ridge High.

She had plenty of classroom experience, so she didn't expect it to be hard to take charge of her students and get them focused on learning. But the subject material was a little iffy.

After teaching English for several years, she was as comfortable with Shakespeare as she was with Hemingway or Shelley or Salinger. Too bad things hadn't clicked into place all that perfectly for this new job. The teacher she was filling in for was a history teacher.

"Do you think you could handle U.S. and world history for a week?" Ava Clayton, the principal, had asked when Danielle arrived for her interview.

"I actually minored in history in college and received a scholastic award from the history department at graduation," Danielle had told the principal. "I've always been interested in history as well as the English language. And I've found that literature reflects the time period when it was written."

Ava had nodded and seemed pleased. "I'll need to make a copy of your educator license and contact the principal in New Loudon for a reference. And then if you're interested, the substituting job is yours."

Now, as Danielle walked into the high school office to introduce herself and pick up the lesson plans prepared by the regular history teacher, she felt a familiar feeling of enthusiasm as she took in the atmosphere that was common to most high schools. Rows of lockers in the hallways. Teachers chatting as they made their way to the classrooms. A couple of early-arriving students gathered outside the building. And a faint mixture of floor-cleaning solution and gymnasium aroma circulating through the hall.

Maybe she could do some good this week. She'd always enjoyed teaching. The only reason she'd given up her job in New Loudon was so she wouldn't have to spend the rest of her life wondering…if only she'd tried to make a go of acting in Hollywood, maybe she'd be another Meryl Streep or Cate Blanchett. The odds were long, but she had to give it a try.

And now she didn't have to wonder anymore.

The first day of teaching went by quickly. She knew she couldn't smile that first day if she wanted to maintain discipline in the classroom. Had to look a bit stern so the students didn't get the idea that she'd be a pushover. And sketching a quick seating chart at the beginning of each class period helped her to connect with the students. She'd found it was always better to call students by their name instead of something like "the boy in the gray shirt" or "the girl with the pink fringe in your hair."

She got home early enough to have a simple dinner ready when Kyle arrived from work. It was nice to be able to tell him about her workday and feel like a professional again.

And by Thursday, when the principal asked Danielle if she could possibly continue the subbing assignment through the following Tuesday because the history teacher needed a few more days to recuperate from surgery, she didn't have to think twice before agreeing.

Kyle acted genuinely happy that Danielle seemed to have found a niche and that the principal seemed pleased with her work. When she greeted him after work on Friday evening, she was excited about a student who'd told her that he wanted to visit the Statue of Liberty after hearing her lesson on reactions of immigrants when they'd first glimpsed the statue while arriving in New York Harbor.

"Now that I've gotten a taste of teaching again," she said, "I think it's as fulfilling as being an actress would be. My taste of Hollywood was probably enough for me. I think I know where I belong."

"Speaking of getting a taste of things, I found a little gourmet shop in town that carries coffee-chocolate chip ice cream." He grinned and held out a brown paper bag with a quart container of ice cream inside. "For those early morning and late-night cravings you've been talking about."

"Kyle, you are so sweet." He did act lovingly toward her. But was he *in love* with her as well? You could act lovingly to your child, your parent, your brother or sister…but that wasn't the same feeling you had when you were head-spinningly in love with someone.

She was so close to feeling that out-of-control, need-to-be-with-him-all-the-time kind of love for Kyle. If only she could loosen that something in her brain that needed to break utterly free.

But how deep did his feelings for her go? She needed to hear it from him.

If his feelings for me really do go that deep.

And then she remembered that night about a week after they'd moved to Cottonwood Ridge when he'd complimented her on the chicken she's made for dinner. He had said the words *I love you* when they talked about her cooking skills. He'd said he loved her no matter how well she could cook.

But she hadn't been sure if he'd merely tossed out the phrase in a casual sort of way. Why did she question Kyle's motivations? His actions showed how he felt about her. She needed to stop analyzing his every sentence and start admitting what she felt for him. Still, she couldn't help wishing he'd say it to her again, so she could see the love in his eyes at the same time.

Then when he mentioned that his parents were eager to meet her but were having trouble scheduling a visit to Colorado, she thought for the tiniest fraction of a second that maybe Kyle was trying to keep her from meeting his parents. Could it be possible that he told her that his parents were happy about the marriage and baby, but he hadn't really spoken to them about it at all?

But that ridiculous thought evaporated as quickly as it had formed when Kyle said his parents had suggested a video chat from their home in Texas on Sunday afternoon.

Unless he was some kind of outrageous impostor who'd hired two middle-aged folks to pose online as his parents, she was actually going to speak to his mother and father in less than forty-eight hours.

* * *

By Sunday afternoon, Kyle sensed an underlying current of tension everywhere in the apartment. He understood Danielle's nervousness over meeting his parents. Even though she didn't know how high they ranked on the list of wealthiest couples in America, it was still unnerving for anyone to meet their husband's folks for the first time.

Especially when the marriage had taken place less than six hours after the couple's initial meeting, the woman had gotten pregnant that same day, and now she couldn't remember a thing about it.

Almost a drive-by wedding.

This was the kind of thing most people would find hard to believe. Hell, he still had a hard time believing it sometimes.

It was crazy, but it was crazy in kind of a good way.

And besides, he hoped to keep some of the

details a little sketchy. Like precisely when he and Danielle had met for the first time.

But he'd been sure to tell his parents that Danielle had no idea of their financial status or their ownership of a successful national restaurant chain. He wanted to be the one to break that news to her. And his father, in particular, had seemed happy to hear that his new daughter-in-law didn't have the makings of what he called a gold digger.

When Kyle prepared to initiate the chat session at two-thirty, he wasn't surprised to notice that Danielle's hands were trembling slightly. Well, his hands were trembling a little bit too.

"They'll love you," he said before he logged in, hoping his voice exuded the proper level of confidence.

And then his parents' faces appeared on his laptop screen, both looking friendly but apprehensive. Even though it was barely past lunchtime, his mother wore her ever-present pearl choker around her neck. That was his mom—classy no matter what the hour or situation.

"Mom and Dad, this is Danielle…my wife." Might as well cut right to the chase. No fooling around. His father probably wouldn't tolerate any dawdling anyway, not with his favorite football team scheduled to kick off their game in thirty minutes.

"It's nice to meet you, Mr. and Mrs. Williams," Danielle said.

"Don't be so formal, Danielle." Kyle's father winked. "Call us Mom and Dad. Hell, maybe you should call us Grandma and Grandpa. We understand there's a baby on the way."

"Bob!" Kyle's mother scolded. "Please excuse him, Danielle. Sometimes he's a little too quick to get right to the point."

"No offense taken." Danielle switched gears and plunged right in to the important part. "I hope you're as excited about the baby as Kyle and I are."

"Are you kidding?" his father cut in. "Kyle's mom here has been bragging to all her girlfriends about it. Believe me, once she gets her hands on that little one, you'll have a hard time getting her to let go."

"Bob, stop scaring Danielle." Kyle's mother's exasperated expression came through perfectly on the computer screen. "Now listen, you two, we've got a lot of things going on with our business right now, and we're sorry we can't get away to visit you yet. But we wanted to tell you that we'd like to furnish the baby's nursery as a gift. Pick out whatever crib you like—"

"And get a nice comfy rocking chair for yourself, Danielle," Kyle's father interrupted. "If that baby is anything like its daddy, you'll be up at all hours feeding it and quieting it down."

"Bob, why do you act like Danielle will do all the work with the baby?" Kyle's mother scolded again. "Now, Danielle, make sure to get a rocking chair that's big enough for both of you to use."

"Oh no, that's much too generous," Danielle protested. "We couldn't possibly accept all that…"

"I hope Kyle didn't tell you not to accept any gifts from us," his father said with a huff. "Sometimes he carries this independence thing way too far."

Kyle fought down the urge to disconnect the chat session. He felt irritation boiling up and consciously took a deep breath to calm himself. His father wasn't bragging about his wealth or anything like that, but he couldn't help feeling annoyed when his father brought up the subject of money. Kyle's refusal to join the family business was a sore that hadn't completely healed.

"Please don't worry, Danielle," Kyle's mother said. She easily stepped into her usual role as the family peacemaker. "Is there anything you need or anything you'd like from us for the baby?"

"Well…" Danielle glanced toward the ceiling, looking to be in thought. "Do you have anything that was Kyle's when he was a baby? Like a teddy bear or a blanket? That would be special to have in the baby's nursery."

Even though it was a digital image on a laptop monitor, Kyle could see it as clearly as if his parents were sitting in the same room with them. They had just fallen in love with Danielle.

If only she could fall in love with him just as easily.

CHAPTER TWELVE

Knowing his parents as well as he did, Kyle wasn't particularly surprised when his older sister called him the next day, asking about meeting his new bride.

His mom and dad had probably told Samantha that they liked Danielle. They'd probably encouraged their daughter to meet the newest member of the family too.

On the one hand, Kyle agreed it was a good idea for Danielle to meet everyone in his family. But on the other hand, the way he and Danielle had met was one hell of a story—and not necessarily a story that he felt was appropriate for sharing with the clan. Especially not with his mother.

And the amnesia thing.

That was one hell of a story too. The whole situation led to the kind of tale you might someday be able to laugh about, but he figured it would take about twenty years for the laughter phase to kick in.

For now, the account was far more likely to be met with astonished stares.

When his sister related that she was in Denver for a medical conference the rest of the week and hoped they'd be able to meet her one evening, Kyle wasn't sure whether to be happy that his family seemed to be welcoming his new wife into the fold or worried that Danielle would let it slip that she still hadn't decided for sure if she'd be sticking around after the baby was born.

Either way, he couldn't avoid a family get-together forever. Even if Danielle didn't want to stay with him, he was still her baby's father and would always play a part in the child's life. And he knew his parents and his sister would want to be involved with his child too. So, they were all going to be connected to Danielle one way or another.

But he knew the way he wanted it to be, and it didn't involve court-ordered visits on specific holidays or occasional weekends. He wanted Danielle one-hundred-percent of the time and one-hundred-percent committed to him. And he wanted to be a full-time dad to their child.

Deciding that he had to forge ahead as though he were certain that Danielle felt the same way, he told his sister that he'd see if they could arrange to meet with her later in the week.

When he got home from work a few hours later, Danielle was buoyed up over her day of teaching but a little sad that the next day would mark the end of her current substituting job.

"The history teacher's doctor cleared him to return to work on Wednesday," she said. "I'm happy that he's recovering well from his surgery, but I've been enjoying meeting the other teachers and working with the students."

"Didn't the principal mention that she might be able to use you as a substitute once in a while?"

"She did. And she also said that her mother-in-law—you know, Sheila the executive housekeeper where you work—had asked if I'd be interested in doing some literacy volunteer work."

"That seems like a strange thing for Sheila to be in charge of."

"Apparently, some of the housekeeping staff and other workers at the resorts in town are learning English as a second language and could use help with their reading skills." She looked at Kyle with questioning eyes. "I think I'd enjoy that, but there's no pay."

"Now I see the connection with Sheila," Kyle said, tapping his temple. "It sounds perfect to me. And I know it would be a big help to some of the employees where I work."

He was struck by Danielle's kindness and compassion, her desire to share her knowledge with others. How could he ever think that she might be primarily interested in his parents' fortune? Other than agreeing to help him out in Las Vegas for a week in order to earn five grand, she never seemed particularly concerned with having a lot of money. She had a healthy desire to have enough money to pay for what was needed, but he didn't recall her showing a bit of interest in designer apparel or any kind of luxury goods.

It was time to tell the truth—the whole truth—

about his family.

"Remember I told you about my sister who's a pediatrician in Dallas?" When Danielle nodded, he continued. "Let's hold off on dinner for a few minutes and sit on the sofa to talk."

"Is everything okay with your sister?"

"Yeah, she's fine." Kyle waved his hand. "She called me today and is super-excited to meet you. In fact, she's attending a medical conference right now at the university in Denver and hopes we could drive over there one evening this week and join her for dinner."

"This week?"

Kyle could see the wheels turning in Danielle's head, and then she perked up and proposed that Thursday night might be perfect. She had an appointment with Dr. Chartoff in New Loudon mid-morning on Friday. Perhaps they could drive separately to Denver on Thursday afternoon, have dinner with Samantha, and then stay in a hotel that night. Danielle could easily drive to her doctor's appointment in New Loudon the next morning, and Kyle could return home to his job at the resort.

With the logistics settled, Kyle regarded his wife levelly. It was now or never. "Before you meet Samantha, I want to tell you a couple of things. She kept a huge secret from my parents, but she lived to tell the tale."

"Meaning?"

"My parents didn't even know she was studying pre-med in college until right before her graduation."

"Why would she keep that a secret from them?

Most parents would be thrilled if their kid wanted to be a doctor."

"*Most* parents." This was it. Now he was going to spring a secret on Danielle. Would she be angry that he'd misled her about his parents? "They thought she was majoring in business so that she could go into the family business."

"Their restaurant?"

"It's not one restaurant. It's a chain of restaurants." He took a breath and plunged forward. "You've probably heard of Uncle Bob's Wild West Steakhouse?"

"Of course. Who hasn't? Wait—is your dad *that* Uncle Bob?"

"Yep." He carefully watched her face, seeing only surprise in her eyes. "My parents started with one restaurant about thirty years ago and built it up to an extremely successful chain."

"Wow, I'm impressed. But what does that have to do with them not wanting your sister to become a doctor?"

"They assumed both Samantha and I would take over their company leadership after they retire. She wouldn't have any part of it, and then they pinned all their hopes on me." He let out a long sigh. "I didn't want to disappoint them, so I felt obligated to study business and hospitality management to prepare to go into the family business. But I changed my mind after college graduation."

"But you can't change your major after you've graduated."

"No, but I changed my mind about working for

my parents. I didn't want any kind of a free ride. I wanted to earn my way, and that's why I struck out on my own."

She studied him carefully. "I'm not sure why, but I have a feeling you told me this when we were in Las Vegas."

He nodded, and his expression brightened. "Right at the end of the week. By then, I didn't think you would care about whether or not my folks were rich. But you forgot about it after your car accident. And then…I'm sorry, but I got a little spooked because of what happened with my former fiancée."

"I thought you told me she left you because she didn't think you earned enough money?"

"That's true. Because she knew all along who my parents were, and she thought I was going to join their business. And that I'd be rich, practically as soon as I graduated from college." He scrunched up his mouth and shook his head. "She didn't love me. She loved the idea of a high-flying lifestyle. And my family's never been like that anyway. My parents are pretty regular people who just happen to have a lot of money."

"They seemed really nice when we had that quick online chat…"

"They actually are. And they do a lot of good with their fortune. Giving back is important to them."

"Your parents sound wonderful."

"That pretty much nails their description," Kyle said. "There's a hospital wing named after them, for all the money they donated. They support quite a few charities."

"I can't wait to meet them in person." She touched her abdomen. "I'm glad our baby carries some of their heritage. And I admire you for wanting to make it on your own."

Our baby. That's what she'd said. He couldn't recall her referring to the baby that way before. Was she forging that connection with him, the coming together of a mass of complicated feelings that resulted in full-on, absolute love?

Now she knew the truth about his family, his financial situation, pretty much everything. And she'd just said that she admired him. But he was sure she hadn't proclaimed her love for him.

Physical attraction, check.

Admiration, check.

But a marriage wasn't going to work without that emotion that was difficult to describe but that people recognized when it hit them.

Love.

He was sure that she'd felt it by the time their honeymoon ended. But could it come back after being wiped out by a head injury?

Maybe it would take root and grow again. But just like with a plant or a tree, that growth wouldn't happen without some nurturing.

"We've got the evening ahead of us," he said to her. "Wanna get out of the apartment and do something fun?"

"What did you have in mind?"

Kyle thought back to the video chat they'd had with his parents yesterday and all the talk about supplies for the baby. "The stores are open until nine. Do you want to go shopping for some things for the baby?"

"That's what you consider as fun?" Danielle tipped her head to the side.

"Spending time with you and planning for our baby—yes, I do." And he was being honest about his feelings.

She smiled tentatively as though in thought, and her eyes glowed as the smile broadened. Moving closer to him on the sofa, she pressed her lips to his. He responded and kissed her deeply.

Kyle put thoughts of Danielle's meeting with his sister out of his mind. That was three days away. Instead, he focused on the rush of love engulfing him.

I think Danielle may finally be feeling the same way about me again.

* * *

Three days later, Kyle had just checked into a hotel in downtown Denver when Danielle stepped into the lobby pulling a wheeled overnight bag behind her. He rushed to her side. "Let me get that for you."

"It's not heavy," she protested. "Putting wheels on these bags was one of the greatest inventions of the last hundred years."

"Tell that to the people who invented television, computers, and spaceships."

"It's called exaggeration, Kyle." Her eyes crinkled as she smiled.

He loved the easy back-and-forth they'd developed. It reminded him of their honeymoon week. Danielle must have felt it too—even if she didn't remember that first week they'd spent together.

"Hey, I want to tell you something." His stomach fluttered, and he knew he had to let her know before they went upstairs to their room. He gripped the key card for the room in his right hand. "They gave us a room with a king bed."

Danielle glanced at the floor for an instant. Then she smiled, and her eyes sparkled. "Should be more comfortable if we want to do some snuggling later."

"I can roll with that." His imagination shifted into overdrive, and he mentally slammed on the brakes. One thing at a time.

When they met his sister Samantha at a nearby restaurant a few hours later, the two women took to each other immediately. They exchanged hugs and acted more like old friends seeing each other for the first time in ten years.

After ordering their meals, Samantha clasped her hands on the table and smiled at Danielle. "So, Kyle told me that you're an English teacher?"

"I was for several years. Then I took a six-month hiatus in an attempt to land a break-out acting role in Hollywood."

Samantha leaned in closer. "How did that work out?"

"Let's just say you won't be seeing me being nominated for an Oscar next year." Danielle shrugged.

"I admire you for pursuing your dream, even if it didn't work out the way you wanted."

Kyle was grateful that his sister didn't press for details when neither he nor Danielle mentioned exactly how they'd met. They had decided to leave any mention of amnesia out of the discussion for now. Why make their story even more complicated?

"I understand the baby is due in early May?" Samantha continued.

"Yes," Danielle said, turning to Kyle. "In fact, we shopped for some baby supplies on Sunday evening." Her face glowed, and she rubbed his arm. "And this guy just had to buy a two-foot tall giraffe for the nursery."

"Sounds like Kyle," Samantha said, laughing and rolling her eyes.

When she offered to help locate a respected obstetrician or pediatrician for them in Cottonwood Ridge, Kyle couldn't help thinking that Samantha had shown the perfect blend of helpfulness and concern without acting pushy.

After dinner when they returned to their hotel room, they embraced and shared a kiss as soon as Kyle shut the door behind them. He encircled his hands around her waist and drew her even closer. "There's something about being in a hotel room with you that reminds me of our honeymoon. And makes me want to relive it."

"I wish I could remember it." Her voice cracked.

"I'm so stupid." Kyle wished he could have kicked himself. "I swore I wouldn't mention memories or anything like that."

"You didn't intend any harm." She stroked his cheek. "Maybe we should focus on making new memories."

"You mean…?"

Danielle nodded her assent, and he guided her to the bed.

CHAPTER THIRTEEN

The next morning, Danielle arrived at Dr. Chartoff's office with a few minutes to spare before her scheduled appointment time. The drive from Denver had been uneventful. With the memory of Kyle's lovemaking fresh in her head from last night, she could almost imagine the world was covered in a rosy glow.

As Danielle entered Dr. Chartoff's reception area, she wondered if the time had come to switch to an obstetrician closer to her new home. A drive of several hours for a doctor's appointment was going to be even more inconvenient when the checkups were scheduled bi-weekly or even weekly in the latter part of her pregnancy.

It made her hesitate, because making an official change of physician implied that she wasn't coming back to New Loudon. Even after what happened with Kyle in their hotel room last night, she still wasn't sure what she wanted to do.

Kyle's family was welcoming to her, and she looked forward to getting to know them better.

And things had changed with Kyle too. Could she truly be falling in love with him again? If she'd actually fallen in love with him after they'd first met on the way to Vegas.

When he'd first shown up at Leslie's door, it was like she'd been told that she was apparently in love with this man, and she was instantly supposed to feel that way because there was a legal document and a baby growing inside of her.

There was no other way to describe that other than it totally freaked her out.

But now, it was no longer something that anyone had to tell her or try to prove from a marriage certificate. Thinking about Kyle made her quiver inside. She couldn't wait to get back to Cottonwood Ridge, so they could be together again tonight.

A greeting from the doctor's receptionist forced Danielle's thoughts back to her pregnancy and her prenatal appointment. After checking in, a nurse weighed her, directed her to the restroom to provide a urine sample, and then escorted her to an exam room where she checked her blood pressure.

"I think Dr. Chartoff will be pleased with your weight gain." The nurse nodded and smiled. "Blood pressure is normal too. And no protein in your urine—that's also a good sign."

After confirming that Danielle was no longer experiencing nausea and hadn't noticed any spotting or bleeding, the nurse instructed her to change out of her clothes into a gown and wait on the exam table for the doctor.

A few moments later, Dr. Chartoff tapped on the door and then stepped into the exam room. “Good to see you again, Danielle. How are you feeling?”

When she reported that her energy level was back to normal, and she felt much better since the occasional bouts of nausea had stopped, the doctor nodded and made a notation in her chart. He had her lie back on the table while he rang a buzzer on the wall to signal the nurse to join them.

Pressing on her abdomen, Dr. Chartoff looked toward the ceiling and appeared deep in concentration. “The size of your uterus indicates the baby is growing at the appropriate rate.” He then explained that he’d be checking the baby’s heartbeat with a fetal Doppler device and gently pressed a small white wand into her belly.

When a rapid rhythm became audible, the doctor subtly winked at her, and Danielle let out a long sigh. Things were looking good. Other than the outward changes to her body, she felt like her old self again. And the doctor’s face didn’t show any sign of concern.

Dr. Chartoff praised her for keeping her weight gain under control. “Gaining the right amount of weight—not too much or too little—increases your chances of having a healthy pregnancy and baby.” He wrapped up the appointment by saying that he’d see her again in a month.

She smiled and simply said, “Okay.” Should she mention to the doctor that she might switch to an obstetrician closer to Cottonwood Ridge? But she still wasn't sure if she should make that official.

Did she need to regain her memories from that missing week before she completely committed to her marriage to Kyle?

What if that never happened?

* * *

After going ahead and setting up the next prenatal checkup with the doctor's receptionist, Danielle sent a short text to Kyle to let him know that the appointment had gone well and then headed to the parking lot. It was early enough for her to stop by Nana's place for a short visit, then have lunch with Leslie, and still get back to Cottonwood Ridge before darkness fell.

With the late autumn sunshine on her face as she exited the medical building onto the sidewalk, she felt an infusion of energy from the warm rays. Energy and a sense of well-being. Dare she hope that the new turn in her life was going to work out for the best after all?

Feeling almost dreamy, she pulled off her light jacket and slung it over her arm, enjoying the unexpected late morning balminess. Her gaze dipped as she reached into her handbag for her car keys, and her dreamlike state quickly evaporated when she spotted a familiar image out of the corner of her eye.

What were the chances of running into Walter Ferguson on an extremely brief visit to New Loudon? And right in front of her obstetrician's office.

Startled, her car keys slipped from her grasp

and bounced onto the pavement.

"Good morning, Danielle," Walter said, bending to retrieve the keys for her. His tone was as formal as speech from a bygone era. Straightening up, his glance traveled up her legs and landed right on her abdomen. "My God, you must be pregnant!"

"Excuse me?" She tried to sound indignant, but anxiety and awkwardness quickly roiled up inside her. She'd known Walter would find out about her baby—and her marriage—eventually, but hadn't considered it urgent to notify him of the specific details of her current situation. After all, he hadn't paid much attention to her since she'd left for Hollywood in hopes of getting professional acting work. Not even when she'd returned to town after her car accident. So, why would he be one of the first people in New Loudon to share in the news?

A crimson blotch worked its way across Walter's face, and his eyes bulged. He opened and closed his mouth three times, as though he were struggling to speak but couldn't find the words.

"I-I guess I made a mistake by not using pr-protection," he stuttered. "But when were you going to tell me?"

"*What*?"

She could almost feel the last drop of blood draining from her head, and the surrounding buildings dissolved into a kaleidoscope of colors and shapes. As her knees buckled, all she could think of was the welfare of her baby.

I can't fall. I can't harm the baby.

Head reeling, she sensed arms clutching her, and the next thing she was aware of was a view of the pavement about a foot from her face. She realized that she was sitting on a bench, bent over at the waist, with her head between her legs. A pair of men's shoes appeared in her field of vision, and the entire incident replayed in her brain.

That must be Walter standing in front of her. What had he just said? Something about not using protection.

What on earth could he be talking about? They'd never had sex. She was sure she would remember if that had ever happened.

Gasping for air, a sensation of déjà vu flooded through her. Finding out she was pregnant. But not remembering having sex anytime recently. Yet having a man claim to be the father of her baby. It was way too much like what happened when Kyle showed up at Leslie's door.

She couldn't possibly have had sex with Walter. He hadn't visited her the entire time she was in Los Angeles. And she was sure it was impossible that he'd somehow gotten into the mix during that week that she was in Las Vegas with Kyle.

When could it have happened? Not after her car accident. She remembered waking up in the ambulance, and her memory was fine after that.

What kind of amnesia did she have? It felt like it conveniently popped up whenever it felt like wiping out a memory.

An even bigger question was what kind of woman she was. Even if she'd been at that point where she still didn't know that she'd married another man in Las Vegas, she couldn't believe she would have slept with Walter right after getting back to New Loudon.

Yes, not long ago, she'd been hoping Walter would show her that kind of attention for quite a while. But he hadn't. Not even close. So, why would she just act without any sense and let him have sex with her without a condom?

Haven't I recently asked myself the same question about the first night I was with Kyle?

But wait, wasn't Walter implying that he'd had sex with her right after her car accident, when she'd been covered with bruises and feeling stiff in a number of places? She was sure she wouldn't have been in the mood for it. Had he forced himself on her?

Why am I not remembering this?

She raised her head and saw Walter gawking at her from above. Struggling to sound adamant, she said, "I'm married to Kyle, and he's the father of my baby."

Walter folded his arms across his chest. "I don't think you can be sure of that."

She'd thought she was sure of it. From what Kyle had told her, it seemed extremely likely. He had a legal marriage certificate. And a believable—well, somewhat believable—story to go with it.

"But—"

Before she could formulate any kind of comeback, Walter cut her off. "Who is this Kyle guy anyway? How much do you even know about him? Can't you see that you and I have much more in common?"

"Maybe we did at one time, but I'm with Kyle

now."

"With *my* baby."

"That can't be true," she protested.

"I say it is." His eyes took on a sly glint, and he nodded. "I came to Leslie's house to visit you shortly after you returned from L.A. She was at work, and you were taking a nap in the living room. I had to keep rapping on the door, and you acted like you were in a fog when you finally answered."

"And then you just..."

"No, of course not," he huffed. "You told me you were having some memory problems. I tried to console you, one thing led to another, and the next thing we knew we were upstairs in your bed."

"Walter, that's ridiculous."

"Ridiculous? You've been chasing after me for years. Ask anybody in this town."

Danielle sniffed. "I was hardly chasing you when I moved to Los Angeles and stayed for six months. And I would've stayed there even longer if I'd been able to land a decent acting job."

"I guess that's what it took to make you realize that you needed to do something exceedingly spectacular to completely get to me."

"Now you're saying this was all my doing?"

"It was entirely consensual, Danielle. You let me know how interested you were and, well, I just couldn't find any reason to hold back."

She fought off a flare of wooziness and rose from the bench. "You're full of it, Walter." Clutching her handbag, she stomped off toward the parking lot, holding her head high in an attempt to project a ton of confidence.

But she was feeling more confusion than confidence. She didn't want to believe Walter, but there was no denying that her memory had some giant-sized holes in it. And he was the second man in recent months who claimed that they'd shared an encounter that had resulted in her pregnancy.

But she'd been a listless mess for the first month after her car accident. Had she somehow perked up barely a day or so after getting out of the hospital and eagerly hopped into bed with Walter?

Was there any way on earth that Walter's story could possibly be true?

She sure wasn't going to annul her marriage to Kyle and turn to Walter. Anyway, she didn't remember Walter saying anything about wanting to marry her. He'd just said that they had a lot in common, but that was about it.

And she knew deep in her heart that she had no interest in being with Walter.

Finally spotting her vehicle in the parking lot, she clicked open the lock and flopped into the driver's seat. What should she do?

She didn't have the slightest idea, but she knew there was only one person who could help her figure out what was best.

CHAPTER FOURTEEN

Not long after that, Danielle showed up at Nana's apartment. She'd told her grandmother she'd try to stop by after the checkup, but she was sure nothing could have prepared Nana for when she recounted her run-in with Walter outside the medical office building.

Nana carefully listened to the entire story and then spoke gently to Danielle. "I know you carry scars in your heart over the way things worked out with your mama."

"What do you mean?"

"It's no secret that she rushed into a marriage with your daddy."

"I never knew the details." Danielle's chest tightened.

"He showed up in town acting like one of those bad boy types, and she couldn't resist him," Nana said. "Then you came along so quickly, and they both loved you so much—they really did. But your daddy had his demons. In the end, he couldn't overcome his addiction problem, and your mama couldn't handle his unreliability."

"But what does that have to do with what's happening with me now?"

"I think it took a heavy toll on you having to see your mama struggle to raise you on her own after your daddy left…and then passed away not long afterwards. And it made you want something different for yourself. A fairy tale marriage, complete with a white picket fence and two adorable tots with smiling faces."

"Who wouldn't want that?"

"It's an ideal, honey. Nobody's marriage is completely perfect, no matter how shiny that white picket fence is. There's good and bad. It's always been that way, and it always will be."

"So, what are you telling me?"

"I think you got this idea that Walter Ferguson is some kind of prototype for the model husband. Because he seems totally predictable. And his family business is well-established, and he seems to be financially secure."

"And you're saying that's wrong?"

"I'm not criticizing the man. He may in fact be the perfect husband—but not necessarily for you." Nana pursed her lips. "Please don't take this the wrong way, Danielle. But if Walter were really interested in you, he would've gone after you in a big way a long time ago."

"But Nana, he says he might be the one who got me pregnant. How could I stay with Kyle if this is actually Walter's baby?"

"Are you seriously going to plan to spend the rest of your life with whichever man got you pregnant? Even if you can't even remember what happened?" Nana gently stroked Danielle's hand, but her eyes showed steely resolve. "You should be with the man who you love. If that man's not the father of this baby, a family court judge can figure out what's best for the child as far as support and custody goes. You'll love this baby and be an amazing mother no matter who the father is."

"And what if Kyle wants nothing more to do with me if it's not his baby?"

"Don't you think you owe him the right to make that decision?"

"Nana, I'm so confused, but I think I don't want to lose Kyle."

"I'm not surprised," Nana said.

"I don't even remember what happened when I first met him. But I think he seemed exciting to me. Ever since I was a teen-ager, I've tried to shy away from guys who seemed like bad boys."

"There's a lot being thrown at you all at once." Nana patted her hand.

"You've given me a lot to think about, and you might be right." Danielle nodded at her grandmother. "Maybe I was trying to avoid what happened to my mother. But something must have made me want to experience that excitement of an adventure with a man who wasn't all prim and proper."

"Honey, I want to clear one thing up. You might find Kyle exciting. But he's not a bad boy. Not in the true sense of the word."

"How would you know that?"

"Remember when you first stopped by here with him? Before he headed over to the hotel near the interstate to register for a room?"

Danielle merely nodded, completely confused as to where her grandmother was going with the discussion.

"And then I told you that I liked him and thought you should take a chance and go with him to Cottonwood Ridge. But I wanted you to text me twice a day, so I'd be sure you were all right."

"Of course, I remember. I've been texting you like clockwork ever since I left."

"Well, you don't think I was going to let my granddaughter run off with a total stranger, did you?"

"But that's pretty much what I did."

"Not exactly. Do you remember when Kyle came back the next week to take you to Cottonwood Ridge, and he said a cop had pulled him over the last time he was in town?"

"Yes, I do remember that. Something about a crooked license plate."

"I don't think the police around here are usually such sticklers for perfect placement of license plates. But I asked my friend, Charlie—you remember, he's the retired chief of police—if he could arrange a legal way for Kyle to get stopped, so that they could run a background check on your young man."

"You didn't!"

"I did. It's what you young professional types call vetting."

"Vetting is for professional jobs, not for potential husbands," Danielle protested.

"Kyle seems to be more than a *potential* husband. Anyway, that's why he got pulled over for the crooked license plate." Nana shrugged as though she were confessing to raiding the cookie jar. "And the check on his driver's license came back clean. No criminal record at all in the national database. So, I could rest a bit easier letting you go off with him."

"Nana, I'm shocked."

"Well, you've done a few things lately that have shocked me, my dear."

Danielle's shoulders sagged. "You're right. I guess I should thank you for looking out for my welfare."

"Isn't that what grandmothers are for?" Nana hugged her. Then her face turned stern, and she pointed her index finger at Danielle. "Now, you need to figure out which of those two men you're in love with—if you're actually in love with either of them. And then you need to find out how important the issue of paternity is to that man. You may end up with no husband at all. Or you may end up with a husband most women could only dream about."

Danielle sighed. "Does life ever get to be simple, Nana?"

Her grandmother shook her head. "No, it doesn't, honey. But it wouldn't be very interesting if it did."

* * *

Danielle settled in her vehicle after leaving

Nana's apartment. She knew that her friend, Leslie, was already planning to meet her for lunch before the drive back to Cottonwood Ridge. But they'd been expecting it to be a final chance to see each other for a while. An opportunity to celebrate what they hoped would be a positive report from Dr. Chartoff that everything was progressing as it should with the baby.

Her head throbbed. Now, she needed to confirm who had actually fathered her baby.

It was going to be embarrassing—make that pointblank humiliating—to repeat to Leslie what Walter said. But she needed to find out about DNA testing, so she'd have to trust her. What other option did she have? Pop in at the local drugstore and ask if they had a DNA test kit that could reveal which of the two men she'd possibly slept with had fathered her baby?

Just imagining having that conversation with the grandfatherly local pharmacist made her break out in beads of perspiration.

So, she took a deep breath and texted Leslie, asking if she had time for lunch. When Leslie replied back that things had been a bit hectic at the hospital and she'd only be able to slip away for a few minutes, Danielle actually felt relieved. That was all the time she needed to spill what she hoped was the last of her outrageous secrets.

Fifteen minutes later, Danielle's heart raced as she and Leslie settled in a relatively secluded area of the hospital coffee shop.

"Did Dr. Chartoff give you a clean bill of health?" Leslie asked, leaning across the table in anticipation.

Danielle nodded. “Everything seems to be progressing normally with the pregnancy.”

“Then why don’t you seem more excited?” Leslie looked at her friend thoughtfully. “Are you and Kyle having problems? He’s not treating you badly, is he?”

“Oh no, not at all. If anything, he couldn’t be nicer to me.”

“I guess it’s hard to pick up and move to a new place twice in the same year.”

“You’re right, it’s rough to leave friends behind, and I miss you.” Danielle put her hand over Leslie’s. “I’ve met a few of the teachers when I substituted at the local high school. So, maybe I’ll eventually make some friends.”

“Well, what is it then? Is it hard to feel a connection to him when you can’t remember how you met him and that time you spent together in Las Vegas?”

Danielle fidgeted. “A little. But I feel like we’re starting to…connect.”

Leslie’s eyes narrowed, and her voice dropped to a whisper. “Have you made love with him again?”

Chewing at her lower lip, Danielle nodded. She wasn’t sure whether to feel embarrassed that she’d gotten so unbelievably intimate with him when she felt she barely knew who he was, or whether to feel even more embarrassed that they were legally married, and they’d only made love twice since moving in together in Cottonwood Ridge.

“So, what’s the problem? Not as good as you

remembered?" Leslie's expression morphed from curious to stricken. "I didn't mean to say that. I should be more sensitive that you don't remember anything about him before that day he showed up at my house."

Danielle lowered her voice to match her friend's. "Making love with him is…divine. But it does seem kind of weird since at first, he was a little like a stranger. A stranger who was very gracious to me, but it's like I got thrown into this super-personal situation with him without even knowing who he was or anything about him."

"Maybe you'll grow to love him again."

"That has actually happened."

"Omigod, I'm so happy for you." Leslie leaned back in her seat and theatrically fanned herself with her right hand.

Danielle glanced nervously around the coffee shop. "Thanks, but I have a bigger problem now."

"But you said that Dr. Chartoff told you everything was fine with the pregnancy."

How could she tell Leslie what Walter was claiming? It was true that she and Leslie had been a little free-spirited on occasion back when they were college girls. But her stomach churned at the thought of telling her best friend that not only had she hooked up—apparently multiple times—with a handsome stranger in Vegas, but she might also have had sex with Walter a few days later. And right in Leslie's house.

It made her skin crawl.

"I-I need your professional opinion about DNA testing. How can I find out right now who the baby's father is?"

Leslie looked puzzled. "Why do you want to do that now? I thought you were going to live with Kyle at least until the baby arrived. And you know that he's the father anyway."

Danielle scrunched her eyes shut, almost as though that would block out the reality of what she was going to say. "Walter," she croaked.

"What's he got to do with this?"

"He says he's the baby's father."

Leslie shrank back. "No!" Then she quickly scanned the coffee shop, as though she were afraid she'd drawn attention to their conversation.

Twisting in her seat to survey the room as well, Danielle then turned back to Leslie and quickly filled her in on the earlier confrontation with Walter. "So, you can see why I've got to find out right away who the real father is," she said when she finished the story.

"It's not that simple." Leslie's brow furrowed. "The only way to do genetic testing on an unborn child is through amniocentesis. They have to insert a needle into the amniotic fluid to get a sample of the baby's DNA."

"That's the only way?" Surely there had to be something less complicated that could be done in this day and age. "I was thinking more of some kind of simple, pain-free swab."

Leslie shook her head and looked alarmed. "No, there's no do-it-yourself test that you could do now to get the baby's DNA. And, of course, you need a sample from the suspected father. But you can't keep this a secret from Kyle. What if your baby is born with a shock of Walter's reddish hair? Can you imagine Kyle's reaction? He'd probably freak out right in the delivery room."

Danielle gulped. "No, I don't even want to imagine that. I hate anything to do with needles, but I think I'm going to have to get the amniotic fluid tested so I can be one-hundred percent sure who the father is."

"I think you should be aware that amniocentesis carries a risk of miscarriage."

"You mean I could lose the baby as a result of the testing?"

"It does raise the chances slightly. That's why it's not routinely done unless there's a strong possibility of genetic defects." Leslie stared fixedly at Danielle. "So, why would you introduce that potential threat to your baby just to confirm right now who the father is?"

CHAPTER FIFTEEN

Danielle got back to Cottonwood Ridge in time to prepare a simple meal of pasta, turkey meatballs, and garden salad before Kyle arrived home from work. That was about as complicated a meal as she could manage, with so many conflicting thoughts ricocheting through her head.

Could Walter possibly be the father of her baby? She had no recollection of anything close to lovemaking happening with him when she'd first returned to Leslie's house—or any time ever, for that matter—but there was no doubt that her memory had some gaps lately.

Maybe she should call the neurologist who'd treated her right after the accident. He should know whether it was possible that her amnesia had continued with some spotty episodes for a few days after the accident. Was it even possible to forget something as momentous as the man you'd been trying to entice for almost two years ultimately taking the bait?

Maybe it hadn't been so momentous.

If it had even happened at all.

But if it *had* happened, she needed to let Kyle know. Otherwise, she was straight-up using him for food, shelter, and medical care during her pregnancy. If he was bending over backwards to take care of her, and then it turned out that she was carrying another man's baby—that didn't play out fairly in any universe.

More than two hours of driving from New Loudon to get back to Cottonwood Ridge and she hadn't figured out how to break the news to Kyle. Because she had to tell him. Even if there was a chance of losing him.

And she didn't want to lose him.

There it was, like a boulder that had landed on her chest, crushing her with the realization that she didn't want to go on without Kyle in her life. It had been an incredibly lucky break when she'd run into him and even luckier when circumstances had all fallen into place to set them up for romance to blossom.

Love had grown from a tiny seed once, when they spent a week in Vegas. And it had happened again when they moved in together and she got to know him again. Since she'd fallen in love with him that second time, her feelings had grown even stronger every day.

When he walked through the door a moment later, a bouquet of daisies in his hand and his face beaming like he was set to hear good news, her heart jumped to her throat. What a good, decent man.

True, the first week of their relationship could be considered by many folks to be on the sketchy side.

But he'd stepped right up to take responsibility for everything he'd done. Besides, not every married couple on earth had first met through notarized recommendations of their family, clergy, trusted friends, or the town mayor. There was that little thing—no, make it a big thing—called chemistry and physical attraction.

And there was no shortage of chemistry or physical attraction between them.

A picture-perfect package of over six feet of manhood with a sense of humor, caring nature, and likeability inside. A package that had landed in her lap when she hadn't even known she'd wanted it.

And now I want to hold on to that package. I don't know how I could possibly live without Kyle in my life.

But she couldn't hold on to him with trickery. Granted, the start to their marriage had been bizarre. Still, if the marriage had a shot to continue, everything going forward had to be based on honesty. Honesty, love, passion, commitment. She wouldn't settle for anything less.

And Kyle didn't deserve anything less.

He crossed the room and held the flowers out to her. "These daisies aren't as beautiful as you are, but they'll have to do for now."

"I can't believe how sweet you are, Kyle." How was she going to tell him what Walter had claimed? If only she could make that whole scenario go away. Walter had dragged his heels about their relationship for nearly two long years. Why did he have to jump in the fray right now, when she'd finally found a man who truly wanted her?

And who she wanted more than anything.

Kyle placed the bouquet on the kitchen counter and then pulled her close to him. "I missed you so much today." In a flash, his mouth was on hers. Not a chaste kiss, but deep and probing. Hungry and longing.

A fiery comet shot straight to her lower belly, and she was ready to invite Kyle to set her alive as he'd done last night in the hotel room in Denver.

She was with the only man she wanted to share that with. Not only did she love the way Kyle could make her feel, she loved everything about the man that he was. If there were rocky times ahead…well, she didn't care. She couldn't remember saying their wedding vows, but she was willing to accept the bad with the good. If they encountered difficult days along the way, she would stand by him.

And yet, every cell in her body that knew the difference between right and wrong was screaming at her that she couldn't keep Walter's claim a secret from Kyle.

Even though when he found out what Walter claimed, Kyle might want nothing more to do with her.

* * *

His lips crushing hers, he couldn't think about anything except making love to Danielle.

Her doctor had said the pregnancy was progressing normally. That's what Danielle had texted after her appointment with Dr. Chartoff. So, there was no physical reason why they couldn't continue to make up for lost time.

He pulled her even closer, certain that she was now aware of his arousal pressed tightly against her belly. Drawing back from the kiss, he placed a hand on either side of her face. "It doesn't have to be hard and furious like the other times. You can have it however you want. Slow and delicious. It's up to you."

Was he imagining it, or had she flinched?

"Maybe you should eat dinner first—" she began.

"I know you put a lot of work into dinner," he broke in. "Maybe we can freeze it for another day? I want you so bad right now. Why don't we order carry-out later?"

The glow disappeared from her eyes. "You may not want to…after I tell you what happened back in New Loudon."

"Not want to—what? Order carry-out?" She wasn't making sense. Didn't she realize how desperate he was to touch her, hold her, become one with her?

Shaking her head, she said, "I think you'd better sit down."

She'd texted him that everything had been fine at the doctor's appointment. No problems with the pregnancy. So, what was she hiding? He hoped nothing had happened with her grandmother.

"Tell me, Danielle."

Her expression was an odd mixture of panic and seasickness. Kyle guided her to the dining table, and they sat down, all thoughts of dinner completely forgotten.

She gasped for air and quickly heaved her breath out. His first thought was that she was supposed to be at the point in her pregnancy where queasiness and morning sickness were no longer problems.

Then she grimaced and blurted out, "Walter says he's the father of the baby."

Kyle's gut clenched, and he was certain that his face had turned three shades of purple. "What the hell? How could that even be possible?"

She sniffled. "He said it was a couple of days after I returned to New Loudon, and he came over to see me while Leslie was at work. When I told him about my memory problems, he tried to console me. He said that one thing led to another. I mean, that's what Walter told me. Apparently, the shock of me coming close to getting killed in a car accident made him realize how he really felt about me, and…well, we might have—"

"Give me a break," Kyle snarled. "Do you even remember this?"

She shook her head, and a flood of tears emerged.

"I thought your amnesia was limited to that period when you left L.A. until you woke up in the ambulance. Now it's selectively kicking in for other incidents? Such as that little weasel supposedly taking advantage of you a couple of days after a serious car accident?"

"I don't think name-calling is going to solve anything."

"You're right. The only way to solve it is to get that damn DNA testing. Find out for certain who the father is. Get that loser—excuse me for the name-calling—get Walter Ferguson off our backs once and for all."

"That *is* the only way to definitively prove who the father is," Danielle said. Her voice quivered. "But it's dangerous to do it before the baby's born."

"What do you mean?"

"I asked Leslie about it. The procedure requires inserting a needle into the amniotic fluid inside the uterus. That's the only way to get a sample of the baby's DNA before it's born. And if we get the testing done, there's a slightly increased chance that I would have a miscarriage afterwards."

"Take a chance on losing our baby just because of that guy's last-ditch effort to steal you from me? No way is that happening."

"Kyle, I'm so sorry."

"Sorry about what? That you slept with the jerk?" He wasn't going to believe that anything had happened between Danielle and Walter. Kyle could believe the amnesia had caused her to forget about meeting and marrying him and everything else they'd done throughout their week together. But even if she had no memory of being married to another man, would she really have so easily allowed Walter to seduce her? And it was crazy that she'd do that while she was still sore from being banged up by the car's air bags.

"Wait a minute," he said. "Walter says he slept

with you a couple of days after your car accident. So, where was he for the next four or five weeks before I showed up at Leslie's door? You and he weren't rendezvousing on a regular basis, were you?"

"No, no," she spluttered, looking horrified. "I'm sure I'd remember that."

A sick sensation lapped at his stomach as he caught sight of the bouquet of daisies, now sitting forlornly on the table. They should be in a vase filled with water. Then he couldn't believe he was concerned about a few cut flowers. An hour before, they'd symbolized the vibrant new start to their intimacy. Now, they signified nothing more than a few objects that had the potential to be beautiful. But instead, they were quickly withering.

Just like his relationship with Danielle.

And what about the baby? The baby that had most definitely bound them together. That's what had convinced her to move in with him, even if she couldn't remember that they were married.

What if the baby wasn't his, after all? He didn't want to believe it. But Danielle didn't seem willing to completely rule out the possibility. How could he deal with the uncertainty of not knowing for sure who the baby belonged to?

"I'll be back later," he said, before he stood up to leave the apartment. "This is way too much to take in. I have to think about it for a while."

She didn't try to stop him.

* * *

Maybe she should have called Kyle on his cell

when he hadn't returned by ten o'clock that night. Maybe she shouldn't have let him leave their apartment in such an emotionally unsettled state. Maybe she shouldn't have sprung such upsetting information on him without laying some sort of foundation.

Danielle thought about it all evening, while she stared mindlessly at the TV screen, nervously clenching and unclenching her hands.

What had she done?

The only man who even came close to showing real love for her had torn out of their home because she might have slept with another man and let him father her child. And she couldn't honestly blame Kyle. Amnesia or not, she couldn't come up with any good justification for her to have acquiesced to Walter Ferguson after returning home from L.A.

The man hadn't even kissed her in more than two years of so-called dating. So, what kind of man would decide it was finally time to have sex when she was only a couple days beyond a serious car accident where she'd briefly lost consciousness?

Not a man who truly loved her.

And even if Walter were that big of a jerk, she had no excuse if she hadn't rebuffed him. Her head injury had wiped out a week's worth of memories, but it hadn't stolen her judgment. Whether she remembered marrying Kyle or not, doing that with Walter at that time was plain wrong on so many levels.

And why couldn't she remember it? She'd been struggling so hard to remember her first meeting with Kyle and everything that happened during the week that followed. And finally, every so often a tiny snatch of recollection wafted to the surface of her memory.

But she wasn't aware of any lingering amnesia episodes after she'd fully regained consciousness in the ambulance. How could she possibly forget having sex with Walter when she had no problem remembering anything else that had happened since the accident?

Had it been so traumatic that she'd hidden it as deep as she could in her mind?

Her throat burned at the thought.

One way or the other, things were messed up pretty bad. Kyle was the man who had demonstrated genuine love for her. Or at least he had been doing that until Walter tried to pry himself back into the picture.

And she knew that her head had been so much in the right place when she and Kyle had ended their honeymoon.

She didn't remember saying her wedding vows, but if the words *for better or for worse, for richer, for poorer* had been uttered, she now knew that she believed in what they meant. And she wanted another opportunity to love and cherish Kyle for the rest of their days.

But she might have squandered her last chance to show Kyle what was truly in her heart. And she was ashamed to face him again.

CHAPTER SIXTEEN

After a fitful night's sleep, Danielle awoke shortly before seven o'clock to the first glimmers of sunrise peeking through the bedroom curtains. The apartment was silent except for the low rumble of the heater.

Had Kyle come home after she'd fallen asleep? Was he still sleeping in the other bedroom, or had he left for work already?

Slipping into her robe, she noted that it still managed to cover her growing abdomen. But not for long. A few more weeks and there would be no denying that she'd need to officially make the move to maternity clothing.

But where would she even be in a few weeks? Kyle might kick her out of the apartment and tell her to let Walter take over responsibility for the baby.

How had she gotten into such a mess?

She gingerly opened her bedroom door, not

wanting to awaken Kyle if he had come home late and was still asleep. But she immediately saw that the door to his bedroom was ajar. She hurried down the hallway and peeked into the bedroom, confirming that he wasn't there. And most likely hadn't slept there either, judging from the totally smooth, unruffled appearance of the bedspread.

Shuffling dejectedly to the kitchen, she flicked on the light and spotted a note on the counter. She focused on the message: *Sleeping at the resort for a while until we sort things out.*

No signature. Definitely no signature signed with love.

Nothing more than an explanation that her husband didn't want to live in the same apartment with her anymore. And probably didn't want to stay married to her anymore either.

She'd thought all along that she was the one with the final say as to whether she and Kyle stayed together as a couple. He'd been acting as though he were willing to go along with it. If only she agreed. Why had he left it up to her?

He must have fallen in love with me during our honeymoon.

A chance meeting, physical attraction, and combustible chemistry had deepened into burgeoning love by the end of that week. Now, she was sure it had happened to her too. But the car accident had wiped away all traces of the experience from her thoughts.

It wasn't fair. If only she hadn't been hit by that car.

The thought suddenly occurred to her that,

considering the force of the collision, she was lucky she hadn't been injured more severely than she was. She couldn't remember that one specific week of her life—a truly meaningful week, to be sure—but she still retained all of the memories that made up her identity. She knew her name, where she was born, all the things she'd learned in school.

And she'd come through the accident with mostly bruises. No broken bones. No internal damage. No loss of the precious baby she'd been carrying inside of her.

Or had she been carrying the baby inside of her at that time? Could what Walter said be true, and had the baby been conceived with him just a few days after that?

A decision suddenly formed in her being. Determining the father of the baby no longer mattered to her. At least not so far as influencing who she loved and wanted to be with. That was Kyle, whether he was the baby's father or not.

She wasn't in love with Walter, she'd never been in love with Walter, and she would never be in love with Walter.

She didn't care if his upholstery business slip-covered every blessed sofa from Maine to California. His dependable income couldn't make up for the feelings that were missing. The feelings that only Kyle could elicit with his sense of humor and adventure, his caring gestures, his tender yet powerful lovemaking.

She'd stumbled on something incredibly wonderful, and now she was afraid she'd let it slip away.

With her thoughts on the baby, she scolded herself for wallowing in self-pity while she should be focusing on the needs of her child. "This baby won't grow like it should if I don't eat properly," she mumbled to herself, heating instant oatmeal and water in the microwave. She opened the fridge to retrieve a grapefruit, placed it on the cutting board, and pulled a knife from the drawer.

A quick slip of her hand gouged the knife into her left thumb, sending a trickle of blood dripping onto the kitchen counter. She pulled a paper towel from the dispenser and pressed it to the cut to stop the bleeding. After a few moments, it stopped, and she delicately washed the blood away at the sink.

"Not too bad," she said aloud to herself, sighing. "Still needs a bandage, though."

She was inwardly criticizing herself for being careless when she discovered there were no bandages in the master bathroom. How long had she been living in this apartment and she still hadn't fully stocked the medicine cabinet?

Maybe there was a box of bandages in Kyle's bathroom. When she opened his medicine cabinet, she immediately found a small box of assorted bandage strips, squares, and circles. Reaching for it, her hand brushed a small, travel-sized bottle on the shelf and sent it sailing to the sink. The top flew off, and the bottle's contents flowed toward the drain.

Fragrance. An eerily familiar scent of men's fragrance drifted into her nostrils and, with it, an image abruptly flashed into her consciousness.

A large bed covered with a snowy comforter. With decorative pillows casually yet purposefully tossed across the top. Rectangular pillows covered in black fabric with a classic Greek key pattern around the edges in gold.

What had her art history professor in college said about the Greek key pattern?

Eternity.

That was it. He'd said it might symbolize eternity. Or eternal love.

As the musky aroma trailed further into her nostrils, an image of Kyle rushed to the forefront of her thoughts. He was in that room with the comforter and the pillows, smiling at her, popping the cork on a bottle of champagne, saying, "To us!"

To us.

Was there still even an *us* to toast?

And as she deeply inhaled the fragrance that burrowed straight into her brain, a series of images briefly hovered in her thoughts. She and Kyle were laughing. They were talking about mysteries and thrillers—yes, they both liked the same kinds of books and films. And he was saying something about wanting to be a success in his own right, wanting to make it on his own.

An unfamiliar sensation caught at her chest, making it difficult to breathe for a second. She wanted to be with Kyle. No matter what they were doing. It was that desire to be with the person you loved for every moment that time and schedules allowed. To tell him about your day, to hear about his day, to share laughter, to cry together if things weren't right, to rejoice in the extraordinary and mundane alike.

I've truly been in love with Kyle all along, but

the car crash temporarily stole my memory of it.

He must have worn the fragrance in the now-spilled container when they were on their honeymoon. But he must not have worn it since then. And it was just like the neurology doctor said. At some point, some—or all—of her memories might be spontaneously triggered by a certain smell, a certain taste, even a certain sound. But the doctor had given no guarantee that anything like that would ever happen.

And yet it had finally happened.

She couldn't give a play-by-play account of the entire week she'd spent with Kyle in Vegas, but she'd just relived enough of it to know that they'd been the real deal.

She'd had everything she could possibly want. And it was gone as quickly as it had come.

* * *

Even though the pillow-top mattresses at the ski resort were considered to be the most comfortable in town, Kyle awoke repeatedly during the night, his thoughts stuck on losing the new family he thought he had, his stomach in knots at the prospect.

Last evening, when he'd arrived home from work with flowers and the hope of rekindling the romantic connection with his wife, he'd been rocked by Walter Ferguson's almost unbelievable claim that he—and not Kyle—was the father of Danielle's baby.

Now, he was kicking himself for running out on her. He'd never been the type to back down, to refuse to stand up to a bully, to settle things any way but fair and square.

But this was an assault of a different type. It was a near-stranger swooping in to steal everything that was most precious to him.

His wife. Their baby.

And did the aggressor even have the right to do it?

Why hadn’t Danielle denied the entire incident outright? She didn’t remember it, but yet she didn’t completely dismiss the likelihood that it could have taken place.

No way she still had lingering feelings for Walter Ferguson. Or was that why she left open the possibility that something *could* have happened with him? Deep in her heart, maybe she knew that she’d be open to Walter if he finally got off his butt and took the next step.

As much as he loved Danielle, he couldn’t remain married to her if she wasn’t truly in love with him.

If she was in love with another man.

But he still cared about her. And he knew that feeling wasn’t going away.

What they’d had together was so different from his experience with his former fiancée. She was a nearly-faded memory, a random blip in his life. A party girl for those fun-loving college days and not all that much of a loss when she threw him over for his buddy. Now, she was no more significant to him than whatever grade he’d received on his first freshman accounting quiz.

It wasn’t the same with Danielle. He wasn’t

going to get over her in a hurry if he lost her to another man.

Stepping into the shower, he tried to let the steamy air clear his thoughts. He should never have let her leave Las Vegas without him. He should have pushed her for a decision right then. Did she want to be his wife, or should they file the annulment papers immediately?

As soon as those opinions formed in his head, he immediately dismissed them. That wouldn't have been the make-all-these-problems-go-away solution. Because he wanted to believe Danielle really had been pregnant with his baby when she left Las Vegas for Colorado. Even if she'd decided the marriage should be annulled, he still would have been responsible for the baby.

Not just responsible, but affectionate and loving too. He wouldn't have been able to walk away from his son or daughter.

Still, the question remained—who was the father of the baby?

As much as he wanted to know, there was no way he was going to allow Danielle to undergo a procedure that might cause a miscarriage, just so they could find out right away who the father was. The risk wasn't justified.

As he toweled off from his shower, guilt overcame him for leaving her alone last night.

Hurrying to the night table, he grabbed his phone and sent a text message to her. Just making sure she was okay. Letting her know he'd stop by the apartment that night to talk. But he wasn't sure if he'd be staying.

That would really be up to her, wouldn't it? She was the one holding all the cards now.

* * *

As Danielle forced herself to eat a healthy bowl of oatmeal, she couldn't help pondering how she'd managed to allow her life to get so messed up. Married somehow, pregnant definitely, but completely confused as to how it had all happened.

Was this some kind of cosmic punishment for wanting a little more out of life than a steady job and a male companion who was into taking her hiking or out to dinner—but nothing more magical or intimate? That had pretty much been the status of her life the last couple of years in New Loudon.

As much as she loved teaching high school English and drama, there was that secret longing deep in her soul to do something out of the ordinary. A secret longing that had pulled her to travel more than a thousand miles from home, all the way to Los Angeles and the lure of Hollywood, just for the chance to show off her acting skills and have some fun while achieving success.

When it hadn't panned out, was it all that surprising that she'd jumped at the chance to feel really alive and bank a lot of cash at the same time? A tingly sensation coursed down through her middle as her thoughts drifted to her initial encounter with a handsome stranger named Kyle who had a money-making proposal.

She pictured him driving across the desert with her at his side, laughing and telling her about the ridiculous plan his boss had dreamed up, and how it was going off the rails because the female co-worker had come to her senses. She could smell that fragrance from the spilled bottle, smell it gently enveloping her in his SUV and beckoning her to join him for a week of fun.

Now, she remembered thinking that maybe she'd gotten the acting bug out of her system. But right next to her was something—someone—who could easily get into her system. And she'd wanted to give him that opportunity.

A ding from her cell phone broke into her train of thought. Her breath caught as she saw a text message had come in from Kyle. Asking if she was okay and if he could stop by for a little while after work.

For a little while...

She took that to mean that he had no interest in staying the night. Even in his separate bedroom. He didn't even want to stay in the same apartment with her.

Could she change his mind? She had to change his mind. There must be some way—she didn't know what it was, but she'd do anything to figure it out—to work things out between them. To prove that she really did love him.

If anything had happened with Walter, she hadn't wanted it. For God's sake, she couldn't even remember it. And it had supposedly happened after her memory-forming capability was entirely back in action. So, it had either been a traumatic event that she'd now blocked out, or it hadn't even happened.

She prayed that it hadn't even happened.

But that could only be proven after the baby

was born. Not unless she wanted to risk a potential miscarriage just to be able to tell Walter that anything to do with her baby was none of his concern.

She couldn't take that chance. Even if she stood to lose Kyle because they couldn't yet be sure who the baby's father was. As much as she wanted to be Kyle's wife, she couldn't jeopardize an innocent life to hold on to her man.

Texting a quick reply to Kyle, she stared numbly at her phone's display screen and reviewed her response. *Yes, and Yes*. She'd simply let him know that she was fine, and she didn't mind if he stopped over after work.

Didn't mind? It was more like she was practically dying to see him. Dying to work out a way to let him know that her memory was slowly coming back.

And the memories were good.

First things first. It wouldn't hurt to make their home seem like a welcoming haven where he'd want to spend time with her. She pulled the vacuum cleaner from the hall closet and ran it over every square inch of floor in the apartment. Then she wiped down and dry dusted every flat surface in the place.

The apartment smelled out-and-out lemony, and she hoped Kyle would take that as a welcoming aroma. But then she thought of another aroma that would be even more enticing.

She could almost hear Nana Rose talking about how it was hard to resist a tantalizing whiff of pot roast. Searching online, she found a recipe that took four hours. There was just enough time to drive to the store for the ingredients and have it ready for Kyle when he walked in. She could only hope that the comfortable atmosphere would relax him enough that he'd be willing to hear about her emerging memories and her wish to start things fresh with him.

With pot roast, onions, potatoes, and carrots jotted down on a sheet of scrap paper, she headed to the local market. By the time Kyle usually arrived home from work, the apartment was filled with traces of mouth-watering scents, there wasn't a visible speck of dust to be found, and Danielle was freshly showered and changed into a casual—but what she hoped was an attractive—outfit of jeans and a loose-fitting tunic.

At a couple minutes after six, a tentative rapping at the front door was followed by Kyle opening it and hesitantly stepping inside. "Smells good in here." The slightest hint of a smile stole across his face.

"Pot roast. I hope you like it."

"It's one of my favorite meals."

Thank you, Nana.

Maybe the comfort food would help to soften his feelings. She checked herself. What was she thinking? Something as serious as his wife possibly getting pregnant by another man, and she thought a plate of beef could make everything right.

No, it wouldn't, but maybe it could help to smooth the way. She had no other options at the moment. "Come on in, Kyle. Do you need to freshen up before we sit down to eat?"

He shook his head. "Just let me wash my hands. I'll use the bathroom down the hall."

Before she could say anything further, he strode past her. No welcoming kiss, not even a dutiful peck on the cheek. Making things right with Kyle was going to take a whole lot more than a meal of meat and vegetables.

He returned to the dining room, looking oddly at Danielle. "How come the bathroom smells like after-shave?"

"Oh, I-I'm so sorry. I was trying to find a bandage after I accidentally cut my finger this morning, and I knocked over a little bottle in your medicine cabinet."

Should she tell him about the memories that had begun flowing along with the stream of liquid fragrance in the bathroom sink? Maybe it was already too late.

Still trying to decide as she picked up the platter with the pot roast and vegetables from the kitchen counter, she carried it toward the table.

"Hey, that looks kind of heavy." Kyle stretched out his hands to take the platter from her. "Let me help."

Releasing her hold to him, she turned to scan the kitchen counter and make sure nothing else needed to be carried to the table. Without warning, a stabbing pain shot through the right side of her torso, powerful enough for her to cry out and clutch the side of the counter.

"What's wrong?" Kyle quickly placed the pot roast on the table and hurried to her side.

"I'll be fine," she gasped between heaving

breaths. “As soon as this pain eases up.”

“No messing around. I’m taking you to the hospital right now.”

CHAPTER SEVENTEEN

"Have you had any bleeding in addition to the abdominal pain?" The triage nurse at the hospital remained calm, but Kyle was sure her face reflected concern as she assessed Danielle's condition.

"No—nothing like that," Danielle said. "Just a sudden attack of searing pain on my right side."

Protectively grasping her forearm, Kyle said, "Don't say *just* when describing your pain. Not when the baby could be at stake." As far as he was concerned, pain that contorted his wife's face the way it had back in their apartment was something to be taken seriously.

"The absence of bleeding is a good sign." The nurse reviewed the notes she'd entered into the computer in the private triage area of the Emergency Department. "And you said your due date is May 8th?"

Danielle and Kyle nodded simultaneously.

"So, the date of conception was roughly…mid-

August," the nurse continued. "And that means you're in approximately the sixteenth week of pregnancy."

Even without any medical training, Kyle knew enough to understand that the baby was way too immature to survive outside the womb.

"That puts you nicely into the second trimester." The nurse cast a glance at Danielle. "I'm going to send you straight to the maternity unit upstairs. There's an obstetrician on duty who can give you a thorough exam. And that's where the specialized equipment is that can help to determine the baby's status. I'll call someone from Patient Transport to take you right up."

As the nurse's fingers flew over her keyboard, Danielle whispered to Kyle, "Didn't you say August 15th was the date we met and got married?"

He nodded absently. That had been the best day of his life thus far. And today had the potential to be the worst day. If anything happened to the baby…

A few minutes later, Danielle sat in a wheelchair on the maternity floor, with Kyle tagging behind as a nursing assistant motioned for the orderly to take her to an exam room part-way down a shiny corridor. Passing by patient rooms, he couldn't help but notice flower arrangements surrounded by teddy bears and balloons. Happiness all over the place.

Would there be teddy bears for their baby? He silently prayed that there would be. And then it clicked—yes, it was definitely *their* baby.

He had been the one right outside the bathroom door when Danielle had found out she was pregnant. The one who'd been at her side when Dr. Chartoff had confirmed the diagnosis. The one who'd scoured the town searching for coffee-chocolate chip ice cream when nothing else would do to satisfy her hormone-driven cravings.

What made a father anyway? A scrap of DNA? Or was it the love, the nurturing, the guidance? Protecting a tiny life from harm and then having the strength to let go when his son or daughter crossed the threshold into adulthood. And being around for the long haul, always ready to lend support in a crisis, no matter how old his child got.

Now that he faced the possibility that the baby might be lost, he knew he wanted—not just wanted, but needed—both Danielle and their child in his life. No matter who had actually contributed the DNA that had combined with hers to create this new life. He wanted to help raise this child.

If Danielle wants me in her life. And in the baby's life.

Sweat seeped from his pores, underscoring his anxiety over the situation. But he had to remain calm for Danielle. As deep as his emotions were running, he knew she had the most at stake right now. The bond between mother and child. It was one of the strongest connections in the entire world, if not the absolute strongest. And she'd already imbibed that potent combination of unconditional love and concern for her baby.

The nursing assistant directed Danielle to a chair in the examining room and then checked her temperature and blood pressure. "All normal," she said, nodding.

He assumed that was a good sign. A fever never meant good news. And he was sure that blood pressure too high or too low could also signal some kind of problem.

"Dr. Sloan will be in to see you shortly," the nursing assistant said, after instructing Danielle to change into a paper gown and sit on the exam table.

No one asked him to leave, so Kyle stayed in the room as Danielle quickly changed and settled on the paper that covered the exam table. It made a crinkling sound, and he wondered if there was anyone alive who associated getting onto a doctor's exam table with fun. Most likely not.

He caught a quick glimpse of Danielle's growing belly and fuller breasts right before she pulled the paper gown completely over her front. That brown line running downward from her navel was still there and even a little darker than when he'd first noticed it.

She sure looked pregnant. How could there be anything wrong with the baby?

Taking in her expression, he could tell that she was frightened. "You all right?" He squeezed her hand and suddenly flashed back to another day in another doctor's office. When they'd first visited Dr. Chartoff for official confirmation of the pregnancy.

Waiting for the doctor to examine her and pinpoint her due date. And that strange feeling of jubilation he'd gotten when the doctor had given them the good news. Kyle had sincerely thought it was good news. In less than two months, he'd found a woman who was smart and dependable, but with the perfect smattering of high spirits. And she'd agreed to marry him, even though it started out as a temporary escapade.

Although it had been an unexpected shock to learn that they were going to be parents so soon into their relationship, he had looked on it as a blessing in disguise. Perhaps the baby would cement their still-fragile bond—a bond made especially fragile by Danielle's memory loss.

So, when she looked at him now with suddenly reddened eyes and whispered, "I don't want to lose the baby," a vise clamped his heart. He loved her so much. The only thing he wanted was to prevent her from being hurt. Even if she didn't want to stay married to him, he didn't want her to experience the heartbreak of a miscarriage.

But he didn't think he could bear it if she didn't want to stay married to him. How had he gotten so wrapped up in her in such a short time? And why wouldn't her brain and her soul let her open her heart to him once again?

He pulled her hands to his mouth and gently kissed them. "I don't want to lose the baby either."

Just then, a woman in a white lab coat with the name *Dr. Sloan* embroidered in red above the breast pocket stepped into the exam room, followed by another woman wearing scrubs. The doctor looked to be in her mid- to late thirties, with intelligent eyes and a comforting smile.

She introduced herself and then took a brief history from Danielle, finally asking her to recline on the table for an examination. Gently palpating the abdomen, the doctor then moved on to an internal exam. Removing her latex gloves and tossing them into the trash can, she smiled at them again. "Everything looks fine with the baby. There's no sign of late miscarriage."

Both Kyle and Danielle seemed to exhale in tandem. "Then what's causing the pain?" Danielle asked.

"It's actually normal to have some aches and pains in your belly," Dr. Sloan explained. "As long as everything else is going fine with the pregnancy, it's usually nothing to be concerned about."

The doctor motioned to a wall poster that showed how the baby grew during each month of the pregnancy. "Right now, your baby weighs almost five ounces and is close to five inches long. Add in the weight of the amniotic fluid that surrounds the baby and the increased weight of the uterus as it expands—well, it can put a lot of extra pressure on certain muscles and joints. As the pregnancy progresses, the ligaments that connect to your bones need to stretch to support your growing uterus. The expanding uterus has a tendency to tilt to the right, and that can cause pain on your right side from spasms."

Danielle's eyes rounded. "You mean this may continue throughout the pregnancy?"

"It may, indeed. In fact, you're experiencing it a little sooner than I usually see. But there are a few ways to deal with it. Just sitting down can sometimes help. Or a warm bath might ease the pain."

Kyle felt a wash of relief that the baby appeared healthy, but he couldn't stand the thought of Danielle experiencing severe pain. "Dr. Sloan, I'm concerned that my wife is having this pain relatively early in the pregnancy. It seems like it might get even worse as the baby gets bigger—like five or six pounds or even more. Is there anything else we can do to prevent an episode like this?"

The doctor looked carefully at each of them. "I don't mean to be overly-personal, but did you have sex shortly before this pain started?"

"Uh, no," Danielle mumbled, her face flushing.

"Well, that can sometimes set off cramping and a mild backache, especially when you get further along into the third trimester." Her assessing eyes swept over both of them. "There's no restriction on having sex as long as everything else is going well. But I recommend that my patients take it a bit slower. Relaxed and easy can still be enjoyable for both of you."

Even though the woman was a physician, Kyle was still embarrassed to be discussing the pace and tempo he should adhere to when having sex with his wife. If he ever had sex with her again. That wasn't a given. The decision was really Danielle's to make.

"Of course, if you experience heavy bleeding at any time," Dr. Sloan continued, "you need to seek medical attention immediately. By the way, who is your regular obstetrician?"

When Danielle told her that she'd been seeing Dr. Chartoff in New Loudon, the doctor looked surprised. "So, you don't live here in town? Were you just visiting here when this pain started?"

"No," Danielle said. "We've moved here recently. I hadn't decided about…about a new doctor yet."

Kyle knew the decision about her doctor was dependent on whether she was staying with him until the baby was born. If not, she'd just go back to New Loudon. But she couldn't be thinking about moving in with Walter Ferguson.

He didn't even want to imagine them together.

And the thought of Walter being the one who wiped Danielle's brow during labor, who brought the newborn home from the hospital, who rocked the baby to sleep at night, so Danielle could get some extra rest—no, it sent a flood of acid churning into his stomach.

He made up his mind that he was going to fight for Danielle. Fight to make her fall in love with him again. Fight to raise their baby together.

If it somehow turned out that Walter Ferguson was the baby's biological father, they'd find a way for him to be involved with the child. But Kyle wanted to be Danielle's husband and the man who helped to tuck their little one in at night. And he wanted to have more babies with Danielle.

If he could somehow make her feel the same way.

* * *

"Have you had your first ultrasound yet?" When Danielle shook her head, Dr. Sloan continued, "The first one is usually done between eighteen and twenty weeks. Dr. Chartoff was probably planning to do it at your next prenatal visit. I'd like to go ahead with it now. It will add that extra layer of confidence that everything is fine with the baby."

"All right," Danielle said. "Dr. Chartoff used a portable device to check the baby's heartbeat—that's it." She followed Dr. Sloan's instructions to wait to be taken to a room with sophisticated ultrasound equipment. Within a few minutes, she and Kyle were in another room with a brown-haired young woman who introduced herself as the sonographer, the technician who would perform the ultrasound.

Danielle quickly sucked in her breath as the sonographer rubbed a chilly gel on her belly.

"Sorry, that's the worst part," the young woman said.

"Is this the test where you find out if the baby's a boy or a girl?" Kyle asked.

"We usually can tell, but it may be a little too early to be sure." She pressed a wand to Danielle's skin and rubbed it over the abdominal area while she checked the video screen. "Do you want to know the baby's sex?"

"I guess so." Danielle figured most expectant couples found out their baby's sex ahead of time. But everything was happening too fast. A few minutes earlier she'd been afraid she was losing the baby. Now, she might know if it were a boy or a girl in just a moment. Her heart ticked faster.

The door to the ultrasound room opened, and Dr. Sloan stepped inside, closing the door behind her. Squinting at the video screen, she said, "Fine healthy baby. Good heartbeat on this little one."

"Can you tell if it's a boy or a girl?" Kyle asked, eagerness showing in his voice.

The doctor moved closer to the screen and paused. "Unfortunately, no. The little angel's hand is positioned absolutely perfectly to prevent us from seeing that part of the anatomy. Well, you'll just have to wait a little longer to find out. I expect that Dr. Chartoff will order another ultrasound when you're further along to check on the umbilical cord, the location of the placenta, and the overall size and well-being of the baby."

It would satisfy their curiosity to find out, but Danielle didn't really care whether it was a boy or a girl. She was head over heels in love with the grainy image on the video screen.

If only Kyle could feel the same way—about both her and the baby.

How could she have ruined things with the most wonderful man she'd ever met?

And when the doctor told her that she could expect to feel the baby's first movement inside of her within the next few weeks, Danielle's feelings were all over the place. She couldn't wait for that thrill of her first real detection of the baby's activity within her. But who would she share it with?

Kyle was with her now to see the first graphic image of the child, but would he even care to place his hand on her belly to feel the fluttering that would soon be taking place?

* * *

By the time they got back to their apartment, it was well past nine o'clock in the evening. Despite the good news about the status of the baby, Kyle was worried about Danielle.

"You must be starving, going all that time without dinner." Even though she protested, saying she'd been too busy to think about food because of all the stress, he insisted on getting her something to eat.

He practically ordered her to change into her nightgown and robe, and then got her situated on the sofa with a pillow behind her back and her feet propped up. When she mentioned an unexpected craving for a veggie omelet, he promised to be back from the diner down the road in a matter of minutes.

Now, as he spread the omelet, buttered sourdough toast, and a cup of strawberries and blueberries on the coffee table for Danielle, he wondered how long he'd be allowed to care for her—and the baby whose image they'd seen only a few hours before.

There was no way of knowing at that moment who had fathered that baby. It no longer even mattered to him. But how did Danielle feel?

Had she been carrying some sort of torch for Walter Ferguson all along? It sickened Kyle to think of the possibility that he'd just been some sort of acceptable substitute, merely good enough if Danielle's true fantasy wasn't available.

He had to lay his cards on the table. If he didn't, Danielle might be gone the next day. Back to New Loudon, back to Walter, taking away everything that had become most important to him. Everything that mattered to him could walk out of his life with barely a backward glance.

He had to find out if she had real feelings for him—not just friendship and respect but full-blown, can't-imagine-life-without-you kind of feelings. She'd found all that with him when they first met. He'd stake everything he owned on the way she'd felt after their first week together.

Yet how she'd felt during their honeymoon didn't matter anymore. Amnesia had taken away her memory of the love that had blossomed—make that exploded—in no more than a week's time. If she couldn't feel that way again, it was going to be hard to convince her to remain as his wife.

But he had to try.

He joined her on the sofa where she was heartily enjoying the omelet that he'd brought from the diner.

"Want some toast?" she asked, holding a slice out to him. "You must be hungry too."

"Nah." He tentatively stroked her belly. Did he still have the right to touch her there? To act protective toward the baby inside? "It's more important for you to eat. Keep your energy up and make sure the baby has all the nutrients it needs."

"I was so relieved when Dr. Sloan confirmed that the baby's developing normally."

"Me too." Their eyes met, and Kyle was surprised to see tears flowing down her cheeks. "What's wrong? You're not having pain again, are you?"

She shook her head and dabbed at the tears with the back of her hand. "I'm happy because the baby's healthy. But…I just wish everything with us was the way it's supposed to be."

"It could be, Danielle." This was the moment to bare his soul to her. Time to tell her what was in his heart. She could accept him or reject him. But he couldn't give up without trying. He'd never been labeled a quitter, and he wasn't going to change his ways now.

"How could it?" She wiped at the fresh onslaught of tears spilling from her eyes. "Not after what Walter said."

Inside his head, the whining of hurricane-force winds drowned out everything else. What he was going to say next was either going to send his life in the direction he desperately wanted—or lead him down a path that he might regret for a very long time. Did he have the courage to say it? Would his family object? Did he even care what his family would think?

Danielle sat waiting for him to respond, her eyes filled with confusion.

His decision made, he brushed her cheek with his hand. "What Walter said—or possibly did—doesn't have to be an issue. I love you, and I still want to be your husband if you'll have me."

CHAPTER EIGHTEEN

Danielle froze, her hand immobilized in mid-air, like some kind of quirky statue holding a slice of toast as a peace offering.

She'd just heard Kyle say that he didn't care if Walter had been the one to father her child. He still wanted to be her husband. And he loved her.

He'd said that he loved her.

What kind of man could put something like what Walter claimed aside? Despite everything, he was willing to let her make the decision as to whether they would continue as a couple.

If you'll have me.

That's what he'd said. She was almost sure of it.

Of course, she'd have him. She didn't want any man but him. Yet how could he possibly feel the same way about her?

Trying to make sense of what she thought she'd heard, she placed her toast with the rest of the food on the coffee table and turned to face Kyle. “I-I’m not sure what you mean. You don’t even care if this is another man’s baby?”

“I want with all my heart for this baby to be the product of the love we shared on our wedding night. But we have no way to determine that until after the baby is born.”

“There *is* a way, but—”

“Not unless we want to put you at risk for miscarriage by getting an amniocentesis done.” He lightly placed a hand on her tummy. “I already love this baby, and I’m not willing to put it in jeopardy just so I can strut around like a proud peacock.”

“But what if we do DNA testing after the baby arrives, and it shows that you’re not the father?”

“I *will* be the father.” His eyes sparked with determination. “Meaning, it doesn’t matter to me whose DNA is in that baby. You and the baby are a package deal, and I want the whole package.”

“I can’t believe what I’m hearing.” Was Kyle truly willing to accept her child as his own even if it had been fathered by a former boyfriend? Or a former acquaintance might be a better description of Walter.

It seemed impossible that he was saying everything she wanted to hear.

“I know you don’t remember any of this,” Kyle said, “but we started as fast friends. It’s true, physical attraction was there right from the beginning. And we did everything way too fast with our super-quick marriage, making love the first day we even met, and probably creating our baby that very night.” He gently drew one of her hands to his lips and kissed her palm. "I so want to believe that you and I created this baby together."

"I want to believe that too," she whispered.

"And I wish you could remember how our friendship and physical attraction quickly grew into real love. The kind you need to keep a marriage going for the long haul. Sure, we're gonna fight. We'll probably have a few problems along the way." He gave her belly the slightest protective embrace. "But if you have the same kind of commitment to me that I have to you—the kind that makes it impossible to imagine going through life without each other—then we'll work everything out."

Her vision blurred, and she realized her eyes were filling with tears again. "There's just one thing you said that isn't right."

"What?"

"The part about me not remembering any of what happened when we first met."

At his expression of total incomprehension, Danielle recounted the minute snatches of memory that had occasionally begun popping to the surface. And the breakthrough that morning, with multiple images forming in her mind, apparently triggered by spilling the fragrance Kyle had worn on their honeymoon.

"When you came in after work tonight, I wanted to tell you what I'd finally remembered. I realized that I actually *had* fallen in love with you during that first week. It was all real, so wonderful and special, and I wanted to be with you more than anything." Her tears spilled again.

"And how do you feel now?"

"I love you, Kyle. You made me fall in love with you all over again." She sniffled. "But I didn't know how to make things right. Not after this whole thing with Walter."

"Screw Walter." Kyle pulled her close to him. "He's not going to mess up the most crazy-special thing that ever happened between two people. If it turns out that he's the biological father—and I don't believe for a minute that he is—we'll see what the courts say about his rights."

"It's scary to think of a judge determining our fate." Danielle's throat tightened.

"Look, if he's entitled to visitation or anything like that, we'll work it out. But as far as I'm concerned, I am this baby's father."

Remembering Leslie's warning about the baby being born with a shock of Walter's reddish hair, Danielle said, "I guess we'll have to do DNA testing after the birth, just so we'll know the baby's true medical history."

"Yeah, that's fine. But in point of fact, I totally love this baby no matter what." He gently kissed the top of her head. "And I feel the same way about the baby's mother."

"How did I just get so unbelievably lucky?"

"No, I'm the lucky one."

She laughed and flirtatiously tapped his chest with her index finger. "Is this one of those fights you just said we're going to have along the way?"

"If it's the worst one we ever have, well, I sure won't complain."

She looked at Kyle, all handsome, all caring, all

saying that he loved her and the baby unconditionally. “I won’t complain if you come to bed with me now.”

“Do you think that’s such a good idea after you’ve just been in the Emergency Department with such bad pain?”

“I mean just to hold me and be with me all night. I want to be as close to you as I can get.”

He met her gaze. “That’s right where I want to be too.”

* * *

Danielle awoke the next morning to the sound of running water coming from the bathroom.

Kyle.

He’d spent the night with her. In the same bed. They’d hugged and kissed and caressed and then fallen into an untroubled sleep.

Not totally untroubled. There was still the issue of scientifically determining who had fathered her baby. But they were going to deal with that and not let it stand in the way of becoming a family.

Even with that dark cloud hovering somewhere in the distance, they’d been able to bask in each other’s love—and be satisfied with passionate embraces for now—while setting aside thoughts of possible legal paternity challenges ahead. They would face any and all hardships together, as husband and wife.

Now, on a lazy Saturday morning, with Kyle not due in to work until lunchtime, the world seemed perfect. Make that about ninety-five-percent perfect. The issue with Walter was still there, but it wasn't going to intrude on the special bond she and Kyle had developed. And she would do whatever it took to make sure that bond was unbreakable.

Danielle stretched, pulled on her robe, and padded to the bathroom. Peeking through the slightly-ajar door, she took in the sight of Kyle, dressed only in jeans, bending over the bathtub. She admired his muscled back. So strong, just like his determination to keep their struggling love alive even when faced with a hail of obstacles.

Making eye contact with her in the mirror above the sink, he turned and let his gaze linger over her mid-section, partly exposed where her robe was gaping open. Raising his glance to meet her eyes, he said, "My God, you're beautiful."

"So are you." What was happening? All she could think about was returning to the bed with Kyle and making their love complete. Kissing yes, fondling yes, but she wanted and needed more.

Kyle turned off the faucet and dipped his wrist into the bath water. "I thought you might like to take a warm bath this morning. In case any of that pain from last night might have returned."

"The pain is gone." She felt nothing but blissful after spending the night snuggled with Kyle. But the idea of soaking in a warm tub for a few minutes evoked images of pampering and being indulged. It wouldn't be that long before she'd be caring for a tiny infant—why not take a few tranquil moments for herself? Besides, Kyle had been so sweet to draw a bath for her the first thing in the morning. "But I like the idea of soaking for a while. I think I'd enjoy it."

She dropped her robe and almost felt Kyle's appreciative glance probing every part of her. His eyes smoldered with desire, and she yearned to feel him against her, inside her. Still, she allowed him to assist her into the tub, and she shifted about until she found the most comfortable position for relaxing.

"I'll make a pot of coffee and bring you a cup," he offered, slowly taking his eyes off her figure, now barely visible through the rippling water.

As he turned for the kitchen, she remembered that she hadn't texted Nana the night before. With all the excitement and apprehension of going to the hospital, she'd forgotten to check in with her grandmother. "Kyle, could you please bring me my cell phone, so I can send a message to Nana? It's on the night table."

He brought her the cell phone, and she tapped out a quick text to her grandmother, assuring her that her health and the pregnancy were fine, and that she and Kyle were working on the marriage relationship.

She left out the specifics. The story of the trip to the hospital could come later. The exact details of how she and Kyle were working to salvage their marriage could be glossed over. But things were mostly good. Ninety-five-percent good, she reminded herself. There was just that one bump in the road still to be navigated. More than a mere bump in the road, Walter Ferguson's claim was an expanding sinkhole that had threatened to swallow their marriage whole.

But it was a threat and not an inevitable event.

She and Kyle would navigate around it. That's what they'd agreed. Putting Walter out of her head, she scrunched down further into the tub, allowing the soothing water to ease the tension from her muscles.

A buzzing from the floor interrupted her descent into complete relaxation. Peeking over the side of the tub, she gasped as she saw Walter's name lighting up the display on her cell phone, now resting on the bathmat.

What could he possibly want so early on a Saturday morning? Danielle's hand quivered as she picked up the phone and clicked on the speaker icon. Was he going to tell her that he'd gotten an attorney to fight for his paternal rights? Could he force her to undergo amniocentesis to confirm which man had truly fathered her child?

She barely managed a feeble "Hello" before Walter's voice assaulted her.

"Danielle? I'm sorry to disturb you first thing in the morning, but I couldn't let this go any longer."

Her heart raced. No one called at an ungodly hour unless it was bad news or some kind of life-changing event. Walter must have some kind of dramatic announcement for her. Details of his plan to cause trouble for her and Kyle—and their baby. She almost called out for Kyle to come back from the kitchen. But how could he protect her from what Walter was going to say and the effect it would have on their lives?

Her throat threatened to constrict to the point where she'd be unable to speak. "What is it, Walter?" she croaked.

"I-I just want to apologize for all the trouble I've caused."

He was apologizing for possibly forcing himself on her and getting her pregnant? A simple apology wasn't going to cut it.

She closed her eyes and inhaled deeply. He couldn't hurt her any further. Or Kyle. Or the baby. She and Kyle were united now. They would face up to whatever needed to be done to do right by their child and protect their marriage at the same time.

"Danielle, are you still there?" Walter's voice tore into her thoughts. "I don't know why I did it—"

"I'm really not interested in your motivation," she cut in.

"You know I'm not the kind of guy who's prone to lying," he continued. "It's just that when I realized you were pregnant, I panicked. I always thought you'd be waiting for me until I decided it was a good time for us to get serious. I was foolish to let my mother dictate how I'd plan my life."

"Walter, what are you talking about?"

"I wanted to move things forward with you, but my mother kept telling me I needed to focus on keeping the family business on track after my father passed away. She said there'd be time later to settle down."

Why was he babbling about his mother? What did she have to do with the sexual encounter that Walter claimed had taken place in Leslie's house after the accident? "I don't understand."

"When I saw you the other day, I just thought of the first thing I could say to try to hold on to you.

I didn't think it through—it came out of my mouth like I was some kind of puppet who couldn't control my own voice.

"Exactly what are you saying?" His mother, the family business, puppets—he wasn't making any sense.

"I made it all up. The whole thing about having sex with you. I never did. It was a stupid attempt to keep you from slipping away."

It had never happened. He'd made the whole thing up.

"I-I don't know what to say." She could barely speak, but she wanted to shout so that everyone within twenty miles could hear her voice. A lingering black cloud had just slipped beyond the horizon, leaving behind nothing but clear skies.

"I guess you told Leslie what I said to you the other day. She tracked me down late last night and pretty much let me know what a Grade A jerk I am. Said I was putting your baby's life at risk because you were going to have a procedure that might cause a miscarriage—just to find out if I really was the father."

"That's right." She *had* been considering the amniocentesis. At least until she'd found out that it could increase the chances of losing the baby. She didn't care how slight the increased risk was—it was a gamble she wasn't willing to take.

"What I said was a spur of the moment, irresponsible grab to try to hold on to you. I had no idea that it could end up putting your baby in danger." The phone crackled and then Walter's voice came through again. "Sometimes you don't realize how special something is until someone else takes an interest in it. I don't blame you if you won't accept it, but I want to apologize to you—and to Kyle—for what I've put you through."

Danielle lifted her gaze from the phone display screen to spot Kyle in the doorway, mug of coffee in hand. "That is not cool, dude," he yelled, his face reddened as he stomped across the room.

With his free hand, Kyle took the cell phone from Danielle. "Man, whatever," he said, and clicked the icon to disconnect Walter's call. After placing the phone and the coffee mug on the bath mat, he leaned down, placed a hand on each of her cheeks, and kissed her.

As the kiss intensified, he worked his fingers through her hair. Danielle grasped his shoulders, not caring if she got him wet, only wanting him to draw even closer to her.

Could it be true? There was no longer any doubt that the baby was Kyle's. The baby was the product of the love they'd shared on their wedding night. No one could stand in their way of becoming a family.

Kyle slowly broke their kiss and focused on her eyes. "It's over. Our second chance at happiness starts today."

She felt a lightness in her chest. "I knew you had to be the father. When the nurse at the hospital said last night that the date of conception was right around August 15th…well, that's our wedding day. And the night you said we skipped the condom. Nothing about what Walter said added up."

"We can forget about him now. He's no more

than a momentary blip on the radar screen." He picked up the mug of steaming coffee and handed it to her. "Go ahead, lean back, and enjoy your coffee while you soak away all the tension from the past few days."

"This is nice. My daily cup of coffee, starting my day with you, and a colossal worry lifted off my chest." A huge mountain of anxiety had just turned into a sea of contentment. "It's clear now that you're everything I always wanted. And I didn't even know what I wanted. But you're definitely it."

Kyle's eyes were all over her. "Seeing you reclining in the water with that mug in your hand...well, it reminds me of when we were soaking in the hot tub in our honeymoon suite. Except now you're drinking coffee with a double dose of cream instead of having a flute of champagne."

Danielle couldn't contain her grin. "Maybe we could do something else to remind us of our wedding night."

"You've got my attention, darlin'." His index finger dipped into the warm water of the tub and traced a slippery but deliberate trail between her breasts and straight down the center of her torso. "But how do you feel?"

"Extremely relaxed. And extremely eager… as long as you follow the doctor's recommendation to go slow and easy."

He pulled a fluffy towel from the rack and helped her out of the tub. After she toweled dry, they impatiently moved to the bedroom. In a matter of seconds, Kyle was out of his jeans and boxers. But once she cozied back on the pillows and he climbed atop her, there was no rush to satiate their hunger.

After they climaxed, they lay entwined for a long while.

"I just remembered something else," Danielle eventually said. "The way you call me *darlin'*. I remember the first time you said it back in Vegas. You said, 'I'll make you glad your car broke down, darlin'.' You said it just before…"

"That's right. And I did make you glad, didn't I? Best-planned car breakdown ever."

"I think when you call me *darlin'*, it means you want to make love to me."

"I think you figured me out pretty good."

"I think this is the start of a whole new life for us," Danielle said.

"I'm in complete agreement, darlin'."

What had he called her?

"Kyle, you couldn't possibly…" She laughed softly, knowing that she would be ready to welcome him whenever he was ready. They were going to have an unforgettable marriage.

EPILOGUE

Two months after Kyle and Danielle welcomed a baby girl, his parents, his sister, Nana Rose, and their dearest friend Leslie all gathered on the spacious deck of the five-bedroom home the beaming paternal grandparents had just purchased on the outskirts of Cottonwood Ridge. The spruce-covered mountain provided the perfect backdrop for simple relaxation or the joyous celebration that was taking place on that sunny July day.

Waiting for Danielle to put the final touches on her make-up and emerge from the powder room, Kyle observed the group from where he stood at the dining room door.

"This will be an ideal second home where we can stay on our occasional visits to see Kyle and Danielle and our new granddaughter," Kyle's dad said. The happiness in his voice was evident. "And all of you are welcome to use the place any time you want to stop in for a visit. There's plenty of room for everyone."

Nana Rose turned to Kyle's father as she lovingly cradled the rosy-cheeked infant in her arms. "I'll be more than happy to take you up on that offer, Bob. It's going to be hard to keep me away from this little porcelain doll."

Just then, Reverend Doug from the community church patted Kyle's shoulder as he passed by and joined the group on the deck. "Good afternoon, everyone. If you'll please be seated, I believe the happy couple will be ready to renew their wedding vows in a few minutes."

Kyle's parents and sister made their way to the three chairs placed slightly to the right, and Nana Rose and Leslie took the two seats just to the left. The infant made a gurgling sound as her great-grandmother settled into her seat, and a collective "Aww" could be heard from the entire group.

"Beautiful baby," Reverend Doug said.

Nana Rose delicately rubbed the baby's chin with her index finger. "Did you hear that, Kyleigh Rose? Everything about you is beautiful."

"Beautiful little girl with a beautiful name." The minister lightly touched the top of her head. "Is there any significance to her name?"

Nana Rose nodded. "It honors Kyle and his family, my late daughter Leigh Ann, and Rose is my name."

Reverend Doug looked at Kyleigh Rose approvingly. "A great deal of thought went into that. Very special indeed." He then took a few steps back as Kyle and Danielle appeared in the doorway that led to the deck, and he nodded at the couple as he opened his book of prayers.

Kyle linked his arm in Danielle's before they stepped onto the deck where six beaming faces greeted them. As he scanned their expressions, he saw joy and approval in their eyes.

Who could have predicted on that day not even a year ago the twist of fate that would bring all of them together today, so that he and his wife could reaffirm their commitment to each other? A car breakdown and a co-worker with cold feet had led to this fantastic new chapter in his life. The beginning of the rest of his life.

He turned to Danielle and took in her fresh-faced beauty, glowing in the same ivory lace dress she'd worn when they'd recited their wedding vows in Las Vegas. A slim-fitting sheath that he'd bought for her at a clothing shop in the lobby of one of the big hotels on the Strip, it flattered the curves that were only enhanced by her recent pregnancy. But now, she complemented the dress with the sterling silver and topaz necklace he'd bought for her at the craft show, with the blue stone perfectly matching her eyes.

This was what complete happiness felt like. The most perfect wife he could imagine, the healthy baby they'd created together, and a family who embraced them despite the questionable start to their relationship.

Locking eyes with Danielle before they began their short walk to stand in front of the minister, he knew that she felt exactly the same way. And although today's ceremony wasn't legally binding as their Vegas wedding had been, it carried a mountain of significance for them.

The first time they recited their vows, it had been with the idea that they were embarking on a fun and exciting adventure for the following week. They'd had no way of knowing how their feelings would change over the course of that week. Or the challenges they would face so early on when Danielle's memory of him was erased by her car accident.

And they'd already been through additional trials, worrying during the early part of the pregnancy about their baby's parentage, and even her survival. But here they were, bound together for life, and ready to face whatever might come their way—as a team, a couple, a loving force that couldn't be broken.

He lightly brushed his mouth against hers, careful not to smudge the subtle wash of lip gloss she'd applied. Then they made their way, arm in arm, to stand in front of Reverend Doug and pledge once more their eternal love for each other. And this time they both fully intended it to be eternal.

I will continue to love you, adore you, and cherish you all the days of my life.

They each repeated the words after the minister, and then exchanged rings. Danielle had assured him she was more than ready to wear the diamond wedding band again. She gasped and then smiled when he slipped it on her finger along with a separate diamond ring with a topaz on each side of the center stone.

When the brief ceremony was finished, Reverend Doug invited them to seal their pledge with a kiss. Kyle didn't need any further prompting, and he kissed Danielle deeply, no longer caring one bit if he kissed away her lip gloss.

The guests on the deck laughed and erupted in spontaneous applause. Kyle and Danielle were quickly surrounded by loving smiles, embraces, and expressions of congratulations.

And when Kyleigh Rose gurgled once again in her great-grandmother's arms, that same collective "Aww" filtered up from the gathering.

Kyle's mother affectionately gave the baby's cheek a gentle squeeze and then turned to Danielle. "I am thrilled with the beautiful name you selected for my little granddaughter. But what about honoring *your* name, Danielle?"

Kyle immediately piped up, "We'll save that for the next baby. I think the middle name will definitely be either Daniel or Danielle."

Nana's eyes glittered. "And when can we be expecting *that* baby?"

"Well, if you'll excuse us, I think we might start working on that project this evening." Kyle grinned and couldn't help feeling playful. "My mom and dad have refreshments for everyone in the dining room, but maybe this is a good time for Danielle and me to head to the honeymoon suite at the resort where I work."

Danielle's face looked apprehensive, and she took Kyleigh Rose from Nana. "I'm having second thoughts about whether it's a good idea for us to be away from her overnight."

Kyle's sister Samantha moved in to pat Danielle's forearm. "You just nursed Kyleigh Rose right before the ceremony, and you've stored more than enough breast milk to get her through the night and tomorrow morning, Danielle. If there's the slightest problem—and there won't be—we'll call you right away. Now, you two go and enjoy yourselves."

His dad nodded vigorously in agreement. "Besides me acting like the proudest grandfather on earth, you have a great-grandmother, a grandmother, an RN, and a pediatrician to help take care of your baby for about sixteen hours. I think they can handle a couple of feedings and diaper changes. The only problem will be when little Kyleigh Rose overdoses on all the hugs and kisses."

Danielle let out a long exhale. "Okay, you convinced me. But I'm sure going to miss her, even if it's just overnight." She placed a kiss on her baby's forehead and slowly handed her back to Nana Rose.

After a few more minutes of hugs and good wishes, the couple made their way to Kyle's SUV, parked in front of his parents' new vacation home. As they clicked their seat belts in place, he said, "I guess this will be a little different from our honeymoon night in Las Vegas."

"Different, but still very special."

Kyle started the engine, and when he glanced over at Danielle, he couldn't help thinking about the last time she'd been in this vehicle wearing the very same lace dress. She returned his gaze, and her expression let Kyle know that they were thinking about the exact same thing.

She smiled and sent him a flirtatious wink.

"Let's go. I want to start building more memories right away."

Then, before they drove to their second honeymoon retreat, she leaned over and kissed him. Kyle swore his heart was overflowing with gratitude for the love and joy they'd both found.

I never want to forget this. And I'll make sure that she always remembers it too.

ABOUT THE AUTHOR

Tina Cambria lives in the Philadelphia suburbs with her family. In addition to writing, she loves to travel, meet new people, dabble in photography, and volunteer for a local hunger relief organization. Her professional background includes nursing, teaching, and information technology.

After leaving the 9 to 5 world behind, Tina followed her dream of writing romance novels. She loves to write about interesting people trying to find love in challenging situations.

Learn more about Tina:
On her website: http://www.tinacambria.com
On Twitter: https://twitter.com/TinaCambria

TINA'S BOOKS

West Coast Christmas Secrets series
A SON FOR CHRISTMAS

Southwest Secrets series ***The secrets start in the Southwest.***
THE HUSBAND SHE CAN’T REMEMBER

Made in the USA
Las Vegas, NV
30 November 2022

60766955R00144